THOSE WHO EAT THE CASCADURA

THOSE WHO EAT THE CASCADURA

Samuel Selvon

TSAR

Toronto

1990

The Publishers acknowledge generous assistance from
the Ontario Arts Council and the Canada Council..

Cover art and design by Natasha Ksonzek.

ISBN 0-920661-12-2

TSAR Publications
P.O. Box 6996, Station A
Toronto, Ontario, Canada
M5W 1X7

For Althea

Those who eat the cascadura will, the native legend says,
Wheresoever they may wander, end in Trinidad their days.

From *History of the West Indies* by Allistair Macmillan

1

Manko put the conchshell to his lips so that it pressed against them like the mouthpiece of a trumpet, and summoned the workmen to the cacao estate with a loud blast. His gaunt cheeks eked out a little elasticity to stretch as he blew: the black of his skin, suffused with pressure and blood, appeared a lighter colour for a few moments, and the lines of age along both sides of his face disappeared into the effort. He closed his eyes as if that helped to power the blast the more, and his head was raised at an angle to the blue sky so that the sound would carry over the tall flaming immortelle trees which were planted to shade the cacao. The long note, at constant pitch to the end, covered the mile to the village, and the cacao-workers bestirred themselves.

The conchshell had come a long way from a fisherman's boat in Mayaro on the south-eastern coast of Trinidad. There, the fishermen used it to announce their catch when the boats came in, and hearing it housewives hurried to the beach to haggle or beg as the case may be. Roger Franklin, the estate owner, was on holiday there once and brought it back to Sans Souci, intending to use it as a door stop. But Manko took possession of it one morning when the original conchshell was misplaced, and had been using it since.

From the kitchen of the big rambling wooden house in which Roger lived and conducted the affairs of the estate, Eloisa, the maid, came out into the brilliant morning to feed the fowls. The cocks had hardly crowed the dawn before the sun settled down on its dreary course for the day. Rising over the hills, it shed golden light like a spendthrift millionaire on the rampage. In no time silver beads of dew evaporated off the grass and bushes around the compound; only down in the cacao a little moisture remained, protected from the fierce heat by the tall umbrellas of immortelle.

'Come, kip. k-i-p!' The call from Eloisa was hardly necessary: the fowls knew the routine, and every morning they gathered in the yard and clucked and clacked impatiently as they waited, and the hens scurried away from the hot cocks as they sneaked up and tried to mount them, pecking at their heads. When a cock succeeded in a mount it spread its wings and the feathers separated and opened out to help it maintain balance, and afterwards . . . only a few moments . . . the hen would give a kind of shudder and ruffle its feathers as if adjusting its dress, and carry on pecking at the ground as if nothing had happened.

Eloisa had an enamel dish of stale boiled rice from which she scooped and scattered as she called. Very soon the fowls were all around her: she turned in a slow circle as she fed them: a few grains fell on the backs of some and before they could roll off others pecked them off. Usually she fed them corn, or chickfeed, shucking the kernels of corn off the cobs if she hadn't had time to do it before, and as her hands filled, flung the corn as if she were sowing a field.

The fowls ate greedily and fought although there was enough for all. By and by they were satisfied and wandered off. There were no coops on the estate: they lived and moved freely, but never strayed from the compound. When the hens laid, Eloisa knew where to look for the eggs, or enjoyed the search. Usually it was under the house, which was elevated about four feet on stout balata posts: otherwise it was in the bushes around the compound. In the evening, they flapped up a ladder Manko had built for her, into a lime tree at the back of the kitchen, and slept there.

Although Eloisa had grown up on the Sans Souci estate, she never liked to wander beyond the immediate confines of the compound. Not even down in the cacao plantation, or to the village about a mile away. Her whole life centred on looking after the house for Mr Roger, as she called him. Beyond the house and the yard, the world held evil spirits, dissension, confusion, and every conceivable badness her imagination could conjure up. Before Mrs Roger died . . . she had forgotten when . . . she used to go away on her afternoon off. She hated the free time when she was thrown on the outside world with nothing to do, no friends to visit,

no place to go. She used to feign illness to avoid her freedom, accustomed as she was to the slant of evening sunlight
on the kitchen window, the murmur of departing workers
from the estate, and the stillness and softness of the evening
as she prepared the last meal of the day. Her slavery had
become a way of life: she never longed for the city of Port
of Spain, or to go to a function in the village. She would
have stoutly denied this was because of her age, or that she
did not have the slippery urges of girlhood after some sixty
five years. But when the manager's wife died she took it upon
herself to run all the domestic affairs, and Roger, in his distress, was glad for her comforting and useful presence. When
he met her . . . when he bought and took over the estate . . .
she must have been old enough to be his grandmother, and
he was forty then. She mothered him, and Gladys too, when
she joined him from England. And when Gladys died the
old black woman wept as it were her own kin. She almost
forcibly kept him observing a period of mourning when he
would have distracted himself in work. 'Mr Roger! Shame
on you! The mistress only bury yesterday and you want
work today! You have to show respect for the dead, else they
come back and haunt you, and pull your toe in the night
when you sleeping! There must be weeping and wailing and
gnashing of teeth, especially as she didn't have a wake, poor
thing. You must stay in a few days and do nothing at all.
I will look after you. And after that, you got to wear a black
mourning band on your arm, to show your sorrow and distress.' He got away from the mourning band, but she insisted
on the few days indoors. Afterwards he was glad she had,
for it helped him to sort out his emotions and think about
what he was going to do. Gladys had been sickly in the
tropics: she did not take well to the heat and the routine
of Sans Souci, and her death was no great shock to him. In
more ways than one it had been a mistake to bring her out
from England: the error had been accentuated by her presence, for he had only married her because he thought she
was pregnant, and when that proved false he came to Trinidad to get away from the dreary burden of living with
someone he didn't love. The estate, at the time, was in a
shambles and fast going to ruin, becoming part of the sur-

rounding bush and jungle, and he had toiled mightily to recover it. It was all he had left now.

Eloisa watched Manko further down the yard as he cleaned his teeth. He had broken a piece of hibiscus and chewed one end to make a brush. Now and then he spat out a bit of the pulp, looking at her and directing his saliva in her direction. He strolled towards her idly, as if without purpose. When he was near he said 'boo' without intonation. Eloisa turned her back on him and folded her arms, looking up at the hills, spurning his presence. They were both so old that the childish gesture seemed ludicrous. For years she had kept up this show of indifference, until it became necessary to display it regardless of any circumstances.

Afterwards they would talk and behave naturally. His 'boo' was not intended for any frightened reaction, it was merely part of the brief pantomime.

She said, turning to face him, 'I got no food for you, Manko, if that's what you after.'

But this too was more pretence. It was like a game they had been playing all their lives. There had been times, through the years, when Manko might have said, 'Look Eloisa, let me and you get married and stop this foolishness. I know you love me.' But the possibility weakened with time, and now it was almost frightening to think of surfacing the reality. Manko used to imagine that only his death would bring Eloisa to her knees. And then, when it was too late, there would be a flood of regret. She would hug and kiss his cold body and try to chaff his limbs to life and wail and gnash her teeth and tell him all the things she should have said while he was alive. And if by some miracle he sat up and returned to life, she would instantly revert to abuse and accuse him of deceit the moment he opened his eyes. Sometimes he wished it could actually happen, just to prove how right he was. It would not be too difficult, with the powers he had, to go into a coma and appear lifeless.

Manko said, leisurely, 'So-o, you going to have company in the house, eh? You will have to do some work for a change.'

Eloisa sniffed. 'Another mister won't make no difference. Doing for two just as easy as doing for one.'

14

'Things not going to be the same when Mr Franklin friend come. You mark my words.'

'Ah, you always divining some stupidness. You could fool the whole of Sans Souci. Excepting me.'

'In any case, what going to happen don't concern you. You is the least of the apostles when it come to that. But other people' . . . he waved the hibiscus toothbrush to indicate them . . . 'going to find their lives complicated. The future is eventful. Prepare for it.'

'Best tell those concerned, then. I not interested in your obeah and black magic. I is God-fearing.'

'What you got for me to eat?'

'Wait here. I will see if anything left over in the kitchen.'

Eloisa mounted the three wooden steps of balata and pushed a swingdoor as she went inside. It closed behind her on oiled springs. It was made of more fine wire mesh than wood . . . as were all the outside doors and windows of the house . . . to keep out insects, particularly the mosquitoes. But the in-and-out traffic gave them ample opportunity to get inside. Every day Eloisa went about the house with a flit-can spraying the rooms. In the evening she lit green coils of slow-burning incense which the local people called 'cock-set.' It came from China and was sold in the shops in little boxes with stands to rest them on. But in spite of these measures the mosquitoes were a constant nuisance.

In the yard, Manko rested against a 'copper' . . . a huge rusty iron basin which was used in the old days to catch water. It was upside-down now, the rim embedded in the earth, forming a dome. Sometimes the estate labourers sat or leaned on it as they waited for Prekash, the young Indian overseer and Roger's right-hand man, to bring out their pay from the office attached to the house. It was smooth and shiny in such places, but otherwise pockmarked like a piece of moon.

The swing-door opened and closed as Rover came out to look at the morning and chase any lingering fowls. As dogs go, it was hard to tell his breed. He might have come from a strain of pothounds . . . the hundreds of stray dogs that roamed about the island, active only when they heard the sound of a pot, denoting food. But Rover had done well for himself since the day he strayed onto the estate and Roger took him in. Like Eloisa, Rover knew when he was on to a good thing and he settled down in Sans Souci to enjoy the comforts of life after years of being stoned and chased by children and irate housewives.

For a moment the animal blinked in the bright light and stretched, bending his spine, front paws pushed out as if he were examining his toenails. Straightening, Rover saw Manko leaning on the copper and froze.

Manko watched the dog with an amused expression. Any moment it would give a yelp of terror and flee, knowing, with animal instinct, that this was no ordinary man, that he possessed powers which were denied others. People knew this too, they called him an obeahman, and said he dealt with spirits. They came to him with their woes and their ailments, asking him to evoke the very powers that frightened them. Had he a different frame of mind he might have exploited their gullibility and made a comfortable living as a practising obeahman. And indeed . . . but purely for his own amusement . . . he costumed his gifts with a certain amount of ritual, knowing the dearth of faith in his fellow men. Instead of taking a bit of logical advice, they preferred him to burn some *veteeveh* bush over a smoky fire and chant incantations. But Manko was not lavish with his gifts. He had spent much time within himself trying to understand what made him as he was, and in the end simply accepted the fact that he had been blessed. He wished he had the intelligence of Rover, for the animal seemed to understand it more than he did. It shunned his presence: he was the only one on the estate to whom Rover did not come running and barking and wagging.

For a little time the dog stared at Manko as if it couldn't believe he was there, a nightmare in the bright sun. And then it whined, tucked its tail between its legs, and slunk off to go behind the house where the view was more attractive.

Prekash came into the shed later that morning, while Sarojini was folding up a mound of cocoabags and putting them away. He stood near the doorway watching her, as yet unseen himself. Of all the sights he had seen that morning . . . the sun, the blue sky, the green hills, the flash of colour as *bluejean* and *pickoplat* flew high in the immortelle . . . none was as Sarojini. Sometimes the poetry that welled up in him as he saw her made him stifle. There was not another girl in the world like this. He looked at pictures in magazines; he peered closely at every other woman he met; he tried to imagine what one more beautiful than Sarojini would look like, and found that his mind was incapable of entertaining such an idea. Amazement and humility filled him when he thought of her, that here in Sans Souci, in a little village in a little island, such beauty could exist. It was like walking in the hills through dense bush and bramble and coming suddenly upon a rare exquisite orchid quite unexpectedly, so that for a moment the senses were stunned. And here, now, in the shed with the musty smell of cocoa, it was as if he lost his reason trying to reconcile her presence in such mundane surroundings. The humility had started as pride that she was his betrothed from the time she was a child. This had been arranged between their parents, as was the Indian custom, and the wedding should have taken place years ago, but Sarojini kept postponing it. He complained to Ramdeen, her father, but he had lost all control over his daughter. Ramdeen blamed Education, and spoke vaguely about the new generation disregarding the customs and habits of their parents.

'But don't worry Prekash,' Ramdeen told him, 'she doesn't love nobody else. You is the onlyest one in the village.'

'Yes, but when?'

'Give she a chance, she will come to her senses soon. She doesn't listen to a word I say, that's the trouble.'

All he could do through the years was live in a world of imagination, consoling himself by turning pride into humility. What a lucky man he was! He did not deserve such happiness, she was far too good for him: perhaps he should be grateful that he saw her every day when she came to work on the estate, and could be near to her, and talk to her. He had dreams that when they married he would lock her up from the rest of the world. She would do no menial work on the estate, or tote buckets of water from the standpipe in the village like the other women. And then he thought maybe he should let the world see this treasure he possessed . . . dress her in the finest silk saris he could buy in Port of Spain; get a jeweller to make her special golden earrings, chains and bracelets; buy a motor car, one of those big fast American ones like those that plied the Eastern Main Road; buy a big house; buy plenty of land; take her on trips to England and America by one of the jets that thundered over Sans Souci on the way to the airport at Piarco. There was fear, too, that all this might not be enough, that no matter what he did for her, he would be falling short of her worth. Perhaps as he showered her with gifts so he could deprive himself and live with the barest necessities to add weight to his love. But eventually, these ambitions became harder to keep alive, until last year when the estate book-keeper left and Roger offered him the job, and also made him an overseer.

'How about it now?' He asked Ramdeen, and bitter with the long wait, 'Unless you want to wait until I take over the whole estate?'

'Is not me you marrieding,' Ramdeen said. 'If you can fix-up with Sarojini, I willing to have you as son-in-law.'

But his promotion seemed to make no difference to Sarojini. For her part, she had dreams too, but not about Prekash. All her life she had been waiting, waiting . . . for what? She did not know. Several times she had been on the verge of saying yes, but each time she hesitated, unable to make a decision. She knew she could have any man in the village, but she did not care for any of them.

Now, as Prekash called her name, she waited for him to go on with the same story.

'You shouldn't be working, Sarojini. When we married, you wouldn't have no hard work.'

'Till then I got to do something.'

'You know it have no need. You just got to say the word and you could live happy in your own house. We wouldn't even have to stay in Sans Souci. How long you going to wait again?'

'Not too long.'

'What you waiting for?'

18

'I don't rightly know. I just can't make up my mind quick.'

'Quick! You call all these years quick?'

'You wouldn't like me to say yes when I didn't want to, would you?'

'But you don't give me no reasons, Sarojini, that's the hurtful part! I not a stupid man. If you could show me cause for waiting, I wouldn't mind. But you going on and on, day after day, year after year.'

'The time not right yet.'

'Who tell you the time not right?'

'Manko.'

'Manko!' Prekash said disgustedly. 'You don't have to listen to him. He ain't no Indian like we. And he got no right in our business. You mean all this time you keeping me in suspense because of some stupidness that man say?'

'Is not no stupidness. You best hads don't let him hear you saying so, before he work an obeah on you.'

'Oho!' Prekash said, slowly and thoughtfully. 'So that's the reason. You believe all that rigmarole Manko does fool people with. I see,' and he nodded his head several times, as if the motion helped him to realize the truth.

'You remember the other day when that baby was sick in the village, and the doctor couldn't do nothing? Ain't it was Manko who give she bush-tea to drink and make she better?'

'Oho,' Prekash was still thoughtful, as if he hadn't heard. What was going on in his mind was patently visible on his face. At first his expression registered slow understanding, as if, the truth discovered, he wanted to savour it and let it percolate. And then there was anger that this flimsy excuse had kept him at bay for so long. And then there was relief that it was such an insignificant obstacle which he could easily brush aside. He found he could smile, and widened it into a laugh.

He was still laughing when Manko came into the shed, so quietly neither of them saw him, Sarojini in the corner with a bag and Prekash's eyes closed as he laughed.

'Like a big joke going on,' Manko observed. 'Tell me so I could laugh too.'

Prekash said without thinking, as if Manko's sudden appearance was in a sequence with what was in his mind,

'What you doing here, Manko, you should be in the cacao helping Ramdeen.'

'I come and go as the spirits tell me. I had a feeling somebody was calling my name and I come to see what it is about.'

'You see!' Sarojini exclaimed, as if she, too, accepted his presence in line with her thoughts.

'You're an old scamp, Manko,' Prekash said lightheartedly, intending to waste no more time now that he knew why Sarojini was keeping him at bay. 'You been fulling up Sarojini head with a lot of foolishness.'

'Foolishness?'

'Yes. Telling she the time ain't right to married! If I wasn't laughing, I would be vex. Work some magic now and tell she we should married at once before it too late!'

Sarojini had moved close to Manko, and she stretched out her hands to him.

'Tell him my fortune, Manko! Read my hands and show him!'

'I don't like to try and convince disbelievers,' Manko said. 'You mustn't play with the spirits.'

'I thought you was my friend,' Prekash said, with mild rebuke, reserving his sarcasm. 'You know how much I love Sarojini . . . you should work your obeah in my favour.'

Manko sighed. 'I sorry for you, Prekash. You going to have a hard time. You going to be called upon to make some great sacrifices. In fact, we all going to have a hard time. Except you, Sarojini.' He pushed her hands away gently. 'I don't have to look there. You going to be happier than you ever was in your life before.'

'What going to happen?' She thrust her hands out again. 'Tell me. Read my fortune!'

'He must be mean you would be happy if we married . . . not so, Manko?' Prekash was pressuring the old man slowly, but he would lose his patience soon.

'I wish it was that, boy.'

'What it is, then?' Prekash was angry now. Suddenly he was frightened that no matter how ridiculous he made Manko appear, Sarojini might be stubborn. 'You better get back to work and stop this idleness, before I cut your pay.'

20

'You wouldn't like to know what in store for you?' Manko mocked.

'It got a lot of stupid people on this estate,' Prekash said, lighting a cigarette and turning away, 'but I not one of them.'

'You frighten for what Manko might say?'

'Who say I frighten?' He blew cigarette smoke to cover his uneasiness. 'You like you run out of excuses and have to fall back on some stupidness this old man tell you.'

'All right.' Sarojini folded her arms. 'If Manko say right here and now that we must get married, I will married. Then you will believe, eh?'

'I know what I want,' Prekash said. 'You is the one who can't make up your mind.'

'I ask you one thing,' Sarojini said impatiently. 'You going to listen to Manko, yes or no?'

'If it will make you happy. But I don't have to believe. Even if it have some men who could tell the future, that don't mean to say they have to be right. Especially a schemer like Manko. I don't know why he had to poke his head in my business.'

Manko ignored him and said to Sarojini, 'You sure you want to know?'

'Yes!' She was like a little girl, already sweetened by the hint of a mysterious happiness.

'Come outside, the both of you.'

They followed Manko into the yard. Prekash puffed his cigarette and yawned. 'Abrakadabra, you full of kaka.'

'Look at the sun,' Manko said.

'You look at it. I don't want to go blind before my time.'

'Watch me.'

Manko looked into the sun, his eyes wide and unblinking. A glassy look was in them, like a blind man.

Sarojini whispered, 'See for yourself Prekash. He looking right inside the belly of the sun!'

'Keep quiet girl.' Manko's head was rigid, only his lips moved. 'Let me concentrate.'

'Ahh.' Prekash tossed his cigarette in a gesture of disgust. 'I not standing up in the hot sun here for this foolishness . . .'

'Listen Prekash!' Sarojini too was as if under a spell, her

whisper excited. 'The birds stop singing! The wind stop blowing! Everything gone quiet-quiet!'

It was an uncanny stillness. If he was uneasy before, Prekash now felt a dread. There was always sound and movement on the landscape . . . the wind in the trees, birds darting in the bush, the glint of a cutlass, the sound of talk and work among the men and women. But for a few moments, as Manko gazed steadily at the sun, it seemed as if the world died. Prekash wanted to move, or say something, but his limbs were lifeless and his voice stuck in his throat.

'All right.' Manko dropped his head. 'Come back inside.'

They followed him back into the shed, and Prekash found his voice in the shade.

'You don't fool me. I know about hypnotism. I seen a man do something like that in Port of Spain once.'

But Sarojini was all concern, fussing over Manko. She spread a bag and said, 'Sit down, Manko, and rest yourself.' And as he did that, dropping down as if the sun had burnt all the life out of him, she pushed out her hands again. 'What you see in the sun? Tell we, Manko, tell we.'

'I don't need your hand, girl. I could read you like a book. I was there the night you born, and your mother dead. Ramdeen never tell you that I warn him your mother would dead and left him alone with you?'

'He never tell me.'

'Let's hear what you got to say, man, so I could show Sarojini how you does lie.'

'I see a lot of the future, but nothing clear as yet.' As Manko spoke, Sarojini leaned forward as if using her whole body to hear. 'I can't give you much details. But girl, you got to watch your steps.'

'Aha!' Prekash flung out his arms as if addressing a crowd. 'What sort of obeahman is this? One minute you say she going to be happy, and the next you warning she to mind she steps!'

'You don't get nothing in life for free. I see a stranger, a white man, who going to make this girl forget everything and everybody.'

'A *white* man!' Sarojini breathed the words.

'Yes. But you got to be cautious, because something wrong with that man. I can't rightly tell at the moment.'

'Try hard Manko, try hard!' In her excitement Sarojini held his shoulders and shook him.

'Is no use. Maybe later, when I see him in the flesh when he come to the estate.'

'He coming right here?' The wonder of it made her back off with her hands to her lips. She could not think.

'Yes. He going to stay for some time. But I see trouble. Plenty trouble.'

'I see trouble too,' Prekash said, using his overseer tone, 'if you don't get back to work. White man!' His voice broke into a grunt of scorn and irony with the last two words. *White man.* He could not make a connection, although the union was suggested.

'As for you, Prekash, nothing good will come. You got to pray under the tree in the village you people have . . .'

'Never mind Prekash,' Sarojini interrupted, as if she feared Manko might forget her. 'Tell me about the man. He good? He bad? What he going to do to me?'

'He is a good man. Though good is good with white people, and is a different thing with black people.'

'I not black Manko!' Sarojini said sharply. 'I is *Indian!*'
'You still black.'

'No!' Sarojini was arguing the point as if it were relevant, as if it would make no difference to Manko's forecast. 'Watch my skin!' And she held out her arm, brushing the fine hairs backwards.

'All that don't make no difference. Black and white will mix until *black is white.*' The last three words, he spoke in the Trinidad acceptance of them, meaning everything would equate.

'Oh, well.' Sarojini saw a collection of circumstance, and was not prepared to analyse or dissect it, as long as her happiness was assured.

'But something funny about him, Sarojini, that I can't see clear.'

'The sun must of make you blind!' Prekash said. 'I never hear so much stupidness in my life.' 'Stay quiet, Prekash!' Sarojini cried, but he went on, 'What I want to know is, when the both of we going to married? That's all I'm interested in. Get Manko to divine that.'

'That is still a mystery,' Manko said. 'A lot of clouds around that time. Wait a minute. I see a ship what that stranger coming on, from far across the sea.'

'And what this stranger name?'

'That I don't know.'

'Well, which part he coming from? The world got names.'

'That I don't know either. But is a big country. Far-far from Trinidad.'

Prekash made a big laugh, and spread his hands as if surprised. 'But you ain't no obeahman, Manko! You mean them little things you can't find out?'

'I only know what the spirits tell me.'

'Sarojini,' Prekash turned to the girl, 'listen. I is a better obeahman still! Because the spirits tell me. He name Garry Johnson, and he coming from England. You can't see old Manko up to his usual tricks? He must of heard Mr Franklin mention about his friend coming to stay on the estate for a holiday, and he making-up this cock-and-bull story to addle your brains.'

'I didn't hear nothing,' Manko said. 'That's how-come I don't know names of people or places.'

'I believe you,' Sarojini said to Manko. 'Don't listen to Prakesh. He only jealous. That's all.'

Prekash laughed shortly. 'Jealous! What I got to be jealous for?'

'What you see again, Manko? Here,' and she pushed her hands again, turning them over and over, as if what one side didn't show the other would. But Manko pushed them aside and got up with an effort, leaving the shape of his bottom in the soft cocoa bags.

'That's enough. It don't do to look too far ahead.'

'I really going to be happy, though?'

'Yes. But I must get a charm for you, to save and protect you.'

Prekash exaggerated his laughter. 'What! Again he saying one thing and meaning another! He going to give you a charm to stop you from being happy?'

'You get the charm, Manko. I will wear it.'

'It will just see that you come to no harm,' Manko rested his hand on her shoulder. 'I got a soft spot for you, girl, being as your father so drunkard.'

She allowed old Manko to touch her, and yet he, Prekash, had to keep his distance. Except he brushed against her accidentally, he had never so much as touched any part of her body. True, he had no reason to suspect she allowed any other man in the village . . . she was even more distant with them . . . but surely he could lay some claim, if only on the duration of his wooing! He was not altogether surprised about her belief that the time was not propitious. Sometimes she displayed this childish innocence, as if she knew nothing, as if she was going to be a child bride and had no idea what her husband would look like, or what he might do to her. He had thought it would be easy to get Manko on his side, after what Sarojini said. He was not surprised she believed him, but he could see her referring to this meeting every time he raised the question of their marriage. He would have to see Manko alone and persuade him to retract his words, or explain that the situation had changed. He did not believe in obeah himself, but if Manko influenced Sarojini, then he would pretend to agree. He might bribe him, although he wasn't sure that would work. But there were things he could threaten him with: he never liked the negro's superior smile: it was enough to fool the superstitious villagers who were scared of a spell or an omen, but he knew it was because Manko was laughing at him because he was too young and inexperienced to be overseer of Sans Souci. They had had arguments about the running of the estate, and the fact that Manko proved right usually, didn't improve the relationship.

He tried now to ridicule the old man. 'You ain't fool me at all. Everything what you say pass through one ears and out the other.'

'You would of sing a different tune though,' Sarojini said, 'if Manko did say I would married you tomorrow.'

'Never mind tomorrow. Right now, the both of you wasting company time. You, Manko, come down in the cacao with me. I want to see what you and Ramdeen been doing. And as for you, you better finish them bags and go help the other women spread the cocoa.'

'Stu-ups,' Sarojini said, making a rude sound, but Manko went with him.

As they left the shed Roger was coming out of the house, screwing up his eyes at the sunlight. He disliked sun-glasses, and paid for it with little wrinkles around his eyes . . . not so much the crow's feet of age as from squinting. He was in his late forties, but years in the sun made him look older: his skin was burnt bronze wherever it was exposed. When he looked in the mirror it was like looking at two men. The parts of his body covered by the khaki shorts and white shirt he usually wore were clearly defined, as if painted white, the rest of him brown and tougher from exposure to the weather. Only his blue eyes picked him out when he was down on the estate with the labourers. Each day he put on clean underwear and freshly-pressed shirts and shorts which Eloisa laid out for him, but this morning she had made him put on long white trousers, as a concession to going to town to meet Garry Johnson. It was a pity he wasn't arriving by plane; then, he would only have had to go to the airport at Piarco, which was much nearer. He never thought of distances in Trinidad from hearsay and traffic signs: often he'd found that the mileage was more, or less, because of the winding roads: even now his mind shrugged at the difference, for the road to town was a highway and he'd have had to bob and weave through cane fields to get to Piarco.

The one long letter he had received from Garry had gladdened him and set up a train of memories. It was more than fifteen years since they met in a Chelsea pub for a farewell drink: his memory of that, was that he had to keep on reminding Garry that it wasn't Jamaica, but Trinidad. Rum for the first, and calypso, *and* cocoa, for the second, before Garry identified. The letter had made no reference to the past . . . it was only long in the sense that Garry was hoping to be able to do some work to keep himself and not be a burden to Roger. It was the only communication he had had from Garry. He had few friends in Trinidad; fewer still who'd take the trouble to forsake the club and the usual crowd in Port of Spain and drive the twenty-odd miles to Sans Souci.

Already he was wondering what he would do with Garry, who might be bored with the estate routine and small village atmosphere. He knew well the preconceptions that people came out from England with . . . glorious days in the sun, sandy beaches and waving coconut palms, natives at their elbows with rum punch and grapefruit. It was an aspect he had no doubt existed, but one which he hardly had time for. From the day of his arrival in the island Roger had had his hands full recovering Sans Souci from neglect and ruin. The bad market for cocoa had made many English proprietors sell up and return to England, or turn to something else. No wonder he'd got the estate at a bargain price, though things had improved since then. He had reason for pride when he thought of what the place had looked like to what he made of it. And the villagers had been happy when he revived the plantation and gave them work. There was little for them to do with the cane farmers, who only employed them during the crop season: the rest of the year they barely existed from their small-holdings and the few stock of animals they kept. He had a good relationship with his men. They treated him with respect, and in spite of independence and the cry to fling the white man out of the country, Sans Souci was divorced from the unrest and strikes that were the birth-pangs of a people moving from subjugation, and he intended to hold out as long as possible.

Seeing the two figures leave the shed, he hailed Prekash, and the young overseer left Manko and hastened over.

'Prekash. You know I'm going to town?'

'Yes Mr Franklin.'

'I won't be long.' Roger glanced about the yard. 'You'd better put some of the women to square up around here, tidy the yard, and give Eloisa a hand in the house.'

'I will send Sarojini to help her.'

'Good. I'll use the Land-Rover. It's got gas?'

'Plenty. I ain't used it, I been using the horse.'

'Everybody out to work?'

'Yes. I got Manko and Ramdeen clearing up the west side, near the river. So much bush there! Maybe you could get some more of that new spray while you in town? We only have a few gallons left.'

'Ah, yes. That reminds me. I must get a mosquito net for Garry.'

Roger started to walk towards the Land-Rover, parked under a mango tree in the yard. It was in such regular use that he never bothered to garage it, like the Austin-seven which he rarely used. He wondered if Garry could drive, it would be useful for him if he cared to roam about the island.

Prekash followed him, unaffected by any thought of freedom from the white man's grip, conscious only that this was a good man who gave him bread and butter, and Roger said as he got in, 'Get someone to pick some of those big juicy oranges, and let Eloisa keep them in the fridge. If I remember rightly Garry loved them.'

'Okay: you wouldn't like a man with you, to help with the luggage and so on?'

'I'll manage.' Roger started the engine, and paused. 'Look. You'd better come over this evening, and have a drink and meet Garry. I won't have much time to spend with him, and you two had better get acquainted.'

'About what time, Mr Franklin?'

'Oh, around eight or so.' Roger, desiring his superiority to be maintained, still hated Prekash's servile attitude: he was always trying to make him feel at ease, to soothe the transition from colony to independent country, but it was a slow job.

Gravel scattered from the back wheels as he drove off: a hen scurried awkwardly out of the way.

As soon as the Land-Rover was out of sight, crossing the small wooden bridge where the river wound through the estate, Prekash went into the office and sat in Roger's chair, swinging his feet and crossing them to rest on the table. By and by, he knew, Sarojini would come to help Eloisa, as was her wont when her estate duties were done. He wished she would be near the office, so she could see him ensconced there, amidst the awesome paper work. Perhaps the telephone would ring and before he could show off his answering it she would be dashing for Eloisa, although the old maid would 'cork her ears' when she heard it on the extension in the house. Eloisa tolerated the electric light and the sewerage, and used the refrigerator and radio. But she could never understand how a person miles away could talk to you and expect you to answer. When Roger had it installed he instructed Eloisa and left a pad and pencil on the small table in the house for her to write down any messages while he was away, but all the pad showed was his own doodling, or odd numbers he scribbled himself.

Prekash swivelled in the chair. At such moments it was impossible for him to forget Sarojini, for it was in this elevated state that he wanted her to be aware of him. And yet, imagining himself king of Sans Souci, he daydreamed as the chair spun on its threaded metal pole, circling him with ambitious ideas. Sometimes working in the office, he deliberately drew Roger's attention so that he would spin in the chair to answer. He observed every slight mannerism, and alone, would assiduously copy every one, holding a pencil in his teeth with both hands, leaning back to blow cigarette or pipe smoke upwards, or just sitting thoughtfully there, swivelling the chair to and fro. In school, Prekash had never had a white man as teacher, but he knew that all the things he was learning taught him to behave as the white man, to think like him, to talk like him, to live like him. And possessing more book knowledge than the other villagers, he had spent a lot of his spare time hanging about the office, so that when the post fell vacant it was natural for Roger to ask him if he would like the office job. But it was lonely with nobody to witness his management, and he took to spreading his promotion to actual duties on the estate, so that he evolved into a sort of overseeing position which Roger did not bother to question. In fact, he was glad for Prekash to take some of the responsibility off his shoulders. Prekash was smart enough not to overplay his hand, especially with an experienced cacao-man like Manko, who was in fact the most knowledgeable of them all. That he made up the paysheets for Roger was enough for the labourers to give him some grudging respect, and it was as much as he could hope for.

There was a little hand-bell on the desk which Roger rang to summon Eloisa. He had others about the house, and they reminded Prekash of when he was in school: he used to like to hold the big one belonging to the headteacher and swing it up and down with both hands, feeling the vibration as the tongue resounded.

He rang the bell now, and opened a ledger and pretended to be scrutinizing it with a thoughful expression as Eloisa came.

'What you arseing around with Mr Roger bell for?' Eloisa stood by the door and did not come in.

'I want a cool drink, Eloisa,' Prekash said, putting authority in his voice.

'What you want is a kick in your backside,' Eloisa said. 'You best hads left Mr Roger desk alone, and go and sit down in your seat in the corner, before I report you when he come back.'

2

The Eastern Main Road is the main artery from Port of Spain to other parts of the island. It runs west to east, changing character from a Yankee-built highway to a narrow strip of asphalt, from city to village and built-up area and bush and jungle and sugar-cane fields. The Yanks were only concerned with getting from their bases to the city, and once past one of these old sites the road deteriorated into what it used to be. It is one of the most dangerous roads in the world because mostly maniacs and madmen drive on it in daily competition for survival. They even carry their own crucifixions and rosaries, prepared to say their last prayers any time, and anywhere, and some dashboards have framed photographs of the driver's family, and others exhibit slogans like 'God is Love' and 'Christ is the Son of Man' and 'Prepare to Meet Thy Doom'. Drivers in Trinidad think they are competent, but they are only lucky. Rabbit's foot and jumbie bead, donkey eye and squirrel tail, save them from disaster. Even the Land-Rover had its *seemeedeemee*, a little bundle of feathers and bones which Manko had put in . . . 'Not for you, Mr Franklin, I know you don't believe in obeah, but it good to let people believe you believe. At the least it will keep out trespassers.' There are gasoline stations and racing pits all along this route: one thing you would never run out of in Trinidad is gasoline, you could never use that as an excuse if you want to stall in some lonely spot with a woman, because 'it got a station just round the corner, who you think you fooling.' As for the pits, they could change a tyre and replace a muffler with your engine running: something seems to go wrong with mufflers in Trinidad, there are special repair shops that do business only with mufflers. Some of the taxis appear to be making their last trip, to the scrap heap, but no, they will chug and rattle and squeak and groan to the bitter end until they literally disintegrate on the highway and cause instant chaos by holding up the flashy models. One such delayed Roger, so that eventually, though he'd planned to do a few things before meeting the ship, he had to forsake the idea and head straight for Wrightson Road where the ships docked.

He had wanted to head back for the estate quickly once the formalities of landing were over, but everything appeared so rushed . . . he'd hardly taken a good look at Garry . . . that he decided to drop in at the club for a drink first. Too, situated as it was around the Queen's Park Savannah, they could take the road through the hills from there and avoid the congestion downtown when they were leaving the city. Roger did not visit the club often: in fact, he kept away from the bridge parties and the beach excursions and the intrigues and opinions. Even with Independence it was still a meeting place mainly, if not exclusively, for whites, and the atmosphere was inevitably patterned like all such clubs fostered by the expatriate English. Few coloured people desired to be members, because they *could* be now, if they wanted. In his early days Roger had had enough of this social life with Gladys, as with local affairs. It was a tricky business to be owner of one of the biggest cacao plantations, and to have lived so long in the island, and yet keep apart from the issues arising from labour and production and other pertinent industrial matters. But once the business was established he employed a firm of lawyers, and a trading company with offices in London, to handle his affairs. Even so there was currently a controversy going on between the sugar and cacao planters which he could not ignore, and which might take up a great deal of his time. He was hoping he would meet one or two of his few friends at the club so that Garry could have some company if he could not spend much time with him.

But it was too early for the place to be crowded. They relaxed with rum punches on the veranda which faced the savannah, with a righthand view of the green hills of the Northern Range.

'Ah, this is better.' Garry sipped his drink with a straw. 'But God, it's hot, even though I crept in by ship.' He was about ten years younger than Roger. They had met during the war and had become close friends, but like many such friendships they lost touch afterwards and had only seen one another once or twice before Roger left for Trinidad. They were almost like strangers now, both reluctant to use the past as a starting point, feeling they were once such good friends that it should be possible to impinge on each other's life and bridge the years casually.

'I'm trying to find out how you contacted me,' Roger said.

'It was all because of a bar of chocolate. I don't usually go for it, but it was pushed on me by a girl I took out one evening.'

'I hope the cocoa came from my estate.'

'Ah, you see the connection? I shoved it in my jacket pocket and didn't think about it until I was taking my clothes to the dry cleaners, and found it had melted and made a sticky mess. One thought led to another as I scrubbed it. You came to mind. I wondered how you were getting on, if you were still in this part of the world where you'd decided to run a cocoa estate.'

'Cacao, not cocoa.' Roger spelt the words. 'Cacao is the tree, cocoa is what you get from it.'

'Live and learn. I've roamed around a bit, with freelance writing. Mainly in Europe and America. I had just come back from a trip to Italy, and the winter was nasty. So, thinking of you out here in the sun, I thought, why not?'

'Just like that?'

'I'm free and single. I never married. Did you?'

'Yes. But let's finish your story.'

'That's it, really. I spoke to my publishers . . . I do those travel things occasionally . . . and they thought I might be able to come back with something.'

'But how did you actually get in touch?'

'Once they agreed I went to the Trinidad Embassy. They told me to try the companies in the cocoa . . . cacao? . . . business, which I did, and eventually got your address and wrote.'

'And what a letter. Merely to give the date of your arrival.'

Garry laughed. 'Well, I'm here now.'

'That's all?'

'You think I'm running from something?'

'You might be,' Roger said facetiously. 'How long you're planning on staying?'

'I'm not allowed to make any plans.' Garry grew serious. He lit a cigarette. 'There's something I ought to tell you, Roger.'

'Ah!'

'It's serious.'

'Oh?'

'You remember my old war wound . . . I sound like a veteran, never mind.' He went on quickly: 'There's still a tiny bit of shrapnel somewhere near my brain and it can't be operated on . . . let me finish. I've tried the best surgeons. Believe me, there's nothing that could be done. One of these days it might shift an infinitesimal fraction and.' Garry snapped his fingers.

'But you're looking so well.'

'Never felt better,' Garry agreed, his tone growing light. 'It doesn't manifest itself in any way. Sometimes I forget about it completely.'

Out on the savannah two boys were flying a common kite . . . one made from a single sheet of paper, diamond-shaped. They were using an old typewriter ribbon for tail. As they played the kite the tail snaked all over the blue sky making loops and figures-of-eight and scrawling fancy patterns. Now and then someone took a short cut across the grass to get to the other side. Almost below the veranda where they sat, traffic plied to and from the business section of the city.

There was a pause because Roger did not know what to say. Garry broke the silence in a bantering tone he had developed to live with his ailment. 'Now we've got that over with, let's forget about it and have another drink. I intend to live to a ripe old age.'

Coming back through the hills, Roger stopped at a lookout point offering a magnificent view of the city and harbour . . . 'A must for every visitor,' he said, 'you ought to see it by night.'

Garry recognized his ship alongside the waterfront, and Roger pointed out a few interesting buildings. When they had ascended on the other side and joined the main road, Garry was tempted to comment when for the third time they had a narrow escape as an overtaking taxi almost forced them off the road. But Roger anticipated him.

'I don't like driving on this road.'

'I can understand that,' Garry said drily.

'Can you drive?'

'Yes. But I think I'll stick to horseback . . . I suppose you've got horses at Sans Souci?' And he went on, musingly interpreting the name, 'Without worry. Did you give the estate that name?'

'It's the village one, but I use it. There are lots of foreign place names in the island. French, Spanish, some from the original Caribs.' He concentrated on the driving for a time. 'I ought to be giving you a running commentary as we go. Those are fields of sugar-cane on your right.'

'That's the main export, isn't it?'

'One of them. The oilfields are in the south. And then there's cocoa. We're having a bit of a bother at the moment. The sugar barons want more land and have asked the government for some of the cacao areas. We've always played second fiddle to cane. Nothing to worry about at Sans Souci, though, but I may be busy while they're sorting it out.'

'What's the estate like? I mean, I've no idea. Do you live in a house?'

Roger laughed. 'Wait and see. It won't be long now, we turn off a little way ahead.'

As they did that he said, sweeping a hand, 'The estate is all around you now. It stretches more than half a mile in any direction this side of the main road. The village itself is about that distance from here.'

They bumped along the rough macadam track as Roger pointed out the cacao trees and the towering immortelles. 'You'll see it all in time for yourself.'

They crossed a small wooden bridge which spanned a shallow branch of the river and drove into the yard. Rover came out of the house, barking. In the yard, Sarojini was making a pretence of sweeping a little distance away. The yard was already clean, but she had been hanging about to see their arrival. And now they were here a sudden bashful-

ness took her and she turned quickly to go away, pulling the
sari to cover her head.

Roger saw her and called, 'Sarojini. Get Eloisa and take
these things inside.'

She had to walk past them, but made such a show of
averting her face that Roger said, 'What's the matter with
you?'

She had to look up then as she mumbled, 'Nothing.' Her
eyes flickered on Garry, and in the swift glance as she
lowered the sari, he felt a shock of wonder. Only afterwards,
when he learnt about her foreknowledge of his coming, did
he understand, but even so it did not explain the sudden,
flooding urge he had to reach out and touch her, and had
even leaned forward to do so. He thought, too, that it might
have been that flash of beauty . . . almost as if her face
radiated a light . . . such as he had never seen in the face of
a woman. Stunned and dispossessed, he glanced at Roger in
a kind of bewilderment and was jolted back to his senses by
seeing him calmly patting the dog. The next moment she was
gone, running and almost tripping over herself in an un-
reasoning panic.

'Who is that?' Garry's throat was dry.

'Rover,' Roger said. 'Here boy, make friends with Garry.'

He laughed to cover up his confusion, and bent to pat the
dog, the misunderstanding giving him the opportunity to
turn his head from Roger's eyes. Never before had he experienced so powerful and instantaneous an emotion. As
they walked towards the house he tried to shake the image
from his mind, and felt that the only way he could do that
was to see her again immediately.

He stopped and said, 'I'll give a hand with the luggage.'

'Nonsense,' Roger said. Sarojini will manage, with Eloisa,
the maid. Let's get out of the sun.' Roger held his arm and
took him inside.

Sarojini, he thought.

Eloisa grumbled as she peeled the oranges. She had her
routine down to a nicety and the visitor had already disturbed a system of movement it had taken her years to evolve.

36

What made matters worse was the threat of his continued presence. Mr Roger had brought back a new mosquito net from town, and the quantity of luggage she and Sarojini had had to lug up the stairs to the bedroom made it look like a long and indefinite stay. It was the hardest work Eloisa had done for a long time . . . Mr Roger should have got one of those hefty idlers, Manko, or that *braggard* Prekash to do it, instead of asking poor Sarojini to tote heavy baggage. She had been nervous and fluttery, twice she dropped things going up the stairs. And no wonder, so like a flower she was, too fragile for the harsh sun and estate labour. She was like a rainbow after rain, and Eloisa knew it would cause trouble some day. She was too beautiful for one woman. It was impossible for ordinary life to spin around this girl, there would be great music and drama and tragedy, one day she would laugh and another day she would cry. In some dim corner of her memory Eloisa remembered a romantic film she had seen in her girlhood, and she likened Sarojini to that grand and awesome world where beautiful people acted out the pageant of life, living in a dream of colour and music, flowers and birds and wind in leafy trees. 'That's the trouble child,' she always sighed when they talked, for like Manko she had great affection for her. 'I try to married you off in my mind, but I can't get anybody what suit you. But you getting big, you know. You not a little girl anymore. When a mango ripe on the tree, if nobody don't pick it it fall to the ground and rotten.'

Her thoughts turned from Sarojini as she started on the sixth orange. How long was this Mr Johnson going to stay, pray? She had missed her usual siesta that afternoon with extra work. Her own home was part of a large extension from the kitchen, two large and comfortable rooms with her own bath and toilet. But the whole house was her proud domain. She could not have been more possessive if she owned the property. She knew every nook and cranny better than Roger himself. For instance, he didn't ever come into the kitchen, or the servant's quarters. Eloisa had the freedom of the whole building and she moved about with the assurance of a titled landlord. Walls of cedar and pillars of mahogany circumscribed her world. There is a smell that pervades in these grand old country houses built from the lumber that grows in the Caribbean. A smell of home and comfort and peace, of kinship and serenity of mind. They are dreamy houses, full of dignity. They have a timelessness about them. Created naturally to live with sun and rain and wind, the wood uses its own strength and durability to repel termite and element. Perhaps yielding a little foothold, a crack here, a little heap of the heart of a post there, like a handful of fine sand, where termites attack. But who would live to see these timbers crumble into dust? All these qualities are discerned more by smell than sight. Eloisa used to say, when the outside of the house was being painted and the posts creosoted, as was done from time to time, that it was sick. During these periods she herself was irritable and fretful and would allow none of the workmen to set foot in the house, not even for a drink of water. By and by, as the rank smell of fresh paint dissipated and the house began to smell its natural self again, Eloisa was harmonized by the scent of teak and cedar, mahogany and balata. Together, they seemed to exude a wholesome, peaceful air from room to room, a friendliness and a companionship. She was never alone, because the house was alive. It was full of laughter and happiness, of memory and a dignified grandeur. These qualities did not necessarily have to have been created with the presence of people at any time: they were rather imagined, sensed by a fine perception, so that a stranger would feel it without knowing any history of the house, or relating his sensations to the linger of dream or fantasy. But it was easy to give full rein to thought of a bygone era, to swirl of hooped skirt or velvet and silk, flirtatious flutter of fan, swaying movement of oldtime waltz, clusters of powdered wigs, deep bows and shooting of laced cuffs, stiff lackeys circling with trays of champagne and wine. There was one concession to the sparking of such reminiscence, imagined or real. It was a tremendous chandelier which hung from the high ceiling in the main room, a giant circular crown of glittering crystal which shot the colours of the rainbow and made gentle tinkling music when wind came into the house. It never failed to mesmerize Eloisa. She avoided looking up at it . . . though she could hardly fail to see it descending the broad stairway which led to the bedrooms. It dazzled her eyes in light or dark, and she would freeze in her passage across the room, or in the midst of some chore, at the slightest tinkle, the merest whisper of a musical note. At such times she was utterly bewitched by the chandelier, confused with dim images of a past she could not recognize or understand. Ghostly figures glided by in a carnival of costume, voices whispered in her ear, and she heard music as if the tinkling signalled an orchestra in the shadows. Once, but once only, she had found herself swaying about the floor in a dance of dream, dispossessed of her feet, in a transport from one side of the room to the other. The experience shook her, pleasant as it was. From that day she clutched firmly to chair or table or banister when the chandelier wooed, or quickened her passage across the polished floor.

She peeled the last orange quickly and flawlessly in spite of her straying thoughts. The yellow skin spiralled off the kitchen knife in unbroken whorls. Her eyes squinted to avoid the tiny flecks of oil which sprung in the process, and which would burn them like peeling onions. Now and again she crisscrossed the blade of the sharp knife on a round stone she had picked up by the river, to sharpen it even more. The spirals of skin she hung by the window to dry: when it became curled and brittle, a small piece would add flavour to cakes and drinks. Sometimes she gave them away to the village children who came hawking, and they set the shrivelled strips of skin alight, to see the oil burn with splutters and flashes of blue and yellow flame, like a firework. They said if you peeled an orange without breaking the skin, and wished, it would come true, and if you tossed it over your left shoulder, you could tell your fortune from the shape it took as it fell.

She had a dozen peeled now, globes of white almost as large as grapefruit. She cut them in halves, sprinkled them with a little salt and bicarbonate of soda so they fizzed, shook a few drops of worcestershire sauce over them, and took them out on a small tray to the back veranda. That was the way Mr Roger, and people who knew their oranges, enjoyed them, and she did not care if Mr Johnson approved. She wondered if the Englishman had ever tasted an orange before.

'I thought you were cooking them,' Roger said when she appeared.

He was sitting with Garry in his favourite evening spot . . . where the veranda curved and widened at the back of the house. From here there was a view of the hills, and a sheen from the bush by starlight which deepened to gold and silver when there was moonlight. Facing out that way Roger felt as if the cares and responsibilities of the estate were indeed negligible. The property extended in a circle all round the house, but at the back here it was quiet and peaceful, with cooling breeze and the sounds of night from the bush. The distant hum of the generator which supplied the estate with electricity was a sound he and the animals and insects had long grown accustomed to, and he was rarely conscious of it.

The mood was so relaxing that they hardly spoke. Garry was sitting in Roger's rocking chair, a rum punch balanced on the flat concrete parapet. He had never sat in a rocking chair before and the soothing comfort of the toing and froing lulled him into a pleasant state of mind in which he had no particular thoughts. He opened half-closed eyes when Eloisa came with the oranges, to find her staring at him.

She put the tray on the small table, shifting the bottle of rum and the jug of ice and glasses to make room.

'You not sitting in the right chair, Mr Johnson.'

The mild rebuke in her tone made him sit up. 'Oh really?'

'Yes. That rocking chair for Mr Roger. Nobody else.'

'It's all right, Eloisa,' Roger said. 'I changed places.'

'You know you like to cool off in the rocker every evening, looking out, with Rover laying down next to you.' The dog, in the corner, growled softly at his name. 'And you didn't put on your *cardigin!*' Her voice rose a pitch. 'I tired tell you that the night air would make you catch cold after all that hot sun in the day!'

Two things she wanted to establish right away. Her relationship with Mr Roger, and that she was not going to run at every beck and call from Mr Johnson. If she put him in his place from the very beginning there would be no nonsense.

'It's not so cool this evening.' Roger gave Garry a broad wink. 'I'm all right.'

'The rum punch was good?' She put the question directly to Roger, turning her back on Garry.

'Lovely, eh Garry?'

'The best I've ever had, Eloisa,' Garry said quickly. 'And as for that sumptuous dinner, I ate so much I can hardly move.'

'My dinners always sumptuous,' Eloisa said, although she didn't know what the word meant, and only guessed its significance. But she was pleased with the compliment. She had gone to a lot of trouble over the meal, but she had to be careful and not let him sweet-talk her into getting the same treatment as Mr Roger.

Garry slammed a mosquito flat on his cheek. Roger said, 'Did you put up the new net for Mr Johnson?'

'Yes. And I light "Cock-set", and left some eucalyptus oil for him to rub down.'

Roger explained what these were, and were for, when Eloisa left.

'What about the mosquito nets, then?'

Roger grunted. 'The bloody things still get in. You can minimize them, but never get rid of them completely, they breed so fast.' He leaned forward and looked closely at Garry. 'You're coming out in bumps already. Try not to scratch them, you'll only make it worse.'

'You seem impervious.' Garry slapped one on his leg and it disintegrated in a smear of blood.

'They like new blood,' Roger grinned. Like the natives, he had built up an immunity. Sometimes on the estate he saw the labourers sitting unconcerned as the tiny blood suckers settled on their skin and became swollen as they filled themselves: a mere brush of the hand then would rub them off to death. He was more irritated by their buzzing.

'Try the oranges,' he told Garry.

For a minute they sucked the fruit in silence. 'They're delicious this way,' Garry said.

'That's how they're eaten here,' Roger said, flinging a piece away from which he had taken a few sucks and moving to another.

'Mother's you, doesn't she?' Garry jerked his head to signify Eloisa.

'She's been with me from the beginning. I couldn't do

without her.' He dropped a piece of orange for Rover. 'Have you noticed she's negroid?'

'Not really.'

'She, and Manko, my old handyman, are the only two on the estate. The others are Indians.'

'Caribs?'

'Lord no. There aren't many Caribs left in the entire Caribbean. Indians who came here originally after slavery was abolished. They make up a large part of the population.'

'You must find it lonely out here.' Garry had had enough oranges, and returned to his drink.

'No.' Roger was emphatic. 'I've enough to do.' He stuffed his pipe slowly, and waved it at the night. 'Look at that. Sometimes I think all the stars in the world meet above this valley. I don't suppose you can hear them yet for the generator, but life is humming and buzzing out there in the bush. Peaceful sounds, in tune with the valley.' He concentrated on getting the pipe going as Garry got up and stood with his hands resting on the parapet, his body inclined outwards as if he wanted to go and see for himself. He made an effort to blank out the steady heavy hum of the generator and pick up small sounds from the forest.

He had done nothing but rest since his arrival, and trade memories with Roger. Already he was relaxed and without care, a state of euphoria he was in no rush to dispel. He breathed deeply the pleasant scent that came wafting down from the hills . . . nutmeg, he thought. He determined not to spare a single moment thinking of London and what he had left behind. He would live for the day each day, taking things as they came.

Roger joined him standing, still in a rhapsody about Sans Souci. 'Some people imagine flowers only grow in gardens on small plants. Wait till you see this place by day. It is a riot of colour, whatever time of year, but some trees are so tall you wouldn't know it unless you kept looking up all the time. I had a bird's eye view one day, from a plane, and it truly astonished me : it was like seeing the valley for the first time. Not a day but some vine or shrub blooms. As for the immortelle . . . ah. Lonely?' He waved his pipe. 'Perhaps. Depends on how you look at it.'

Behind them Rover got up and went to the top of the back steps, where he pointed and growled.

'Must be Prekash,' Roger said. 'My young overseer.'

Garry looked down and sideways, and saw Prekash as he came into the light and began to come up the steps.

It was Prekash's first social visit to the house, and he was rankled because that old black bitch had made him use the back steps, as if he were selling mangoes or fish. He had put on clean clothes and was looking forward to a grand entry, ushered in and offered a seat and a choice of drinks. Instead, he had to stumble in the dark, and he forgot the bird pepper tree and soiled his white shirt brushing against it.

'Forget the "Mr Johnson",' Garry said when they were introduced.

'And help yourself to a drink,' Roger waved him to the table. He always tried to put Prekash at ease, but there was always a great fear in Prekash that he might endanger his job if he became too familiar. The invitation to visit had him nervous at first, but after he had fired a few drinks in the shop to calm himself, he boasted to his friends that Mr Franklin was beginning to treat him as an equal. They all thought he was lying, that it was a matter of discussing business. But he smiled to himself, one day they would find out. It was always *one day* with him, some nebulous date in the future when things would go right for him. Coming from the village, he thought about this white stranger who was going to cause trouble with Sarojini, and approached the house with some vague intention of establishing his rights at the outset. He would be respectful, but at the same time firm and confident. Now, after the encounter with Eloisa, his resolution was in pieces and he badly needed a drink. *Talk man talk*, he told himself turning from the table, *make conversation. What you frighten for?*

'You had a good trip, Mr . . . Garry?'

'Wonderful. Nothing like a sea voyage for rest and peace.'

'Most people who come, come by plane. The airport at Piarco not far from here, you know. We see jets coming and going all the time.' He spoke all this quickly, and shot the rum down with a jerk of his hand, like a dusty cowboy in a new town. He grabbed the bottle and poured another before

Mr Franklin could thunder: *Leave that rum alone, who do you think you are?*

'Fill up your glass and relax,' Roger said.

'One thing I long to see more than anything else,' Prekash said, 'Snow.'

'I've had my fill of that. I've come for some sun.'

'What it look like? Mr Franklin tell me it like shave-ice.'

'Shave-ice?'

'Vendors shave blocks of ice . . . like planing a piece of wood,' Roger explained. 'They make a sort of ice lolly with it.'

'What I don't understand is how it fall from the sky, like rain.' Prekash's nervousness was fast disappearing as the rum coursed through his veins.

'Yes. Well, I've got some pictures, Prekash. I'll show you some time.'

'It sound like obeah to me, all that whiteness falling down.'

'Ah, obeah.' Garry looked at Roger. 'It's something I'm interested in. Perhaps I could get some material for a book?'

Roger puffed his pipe. 'No shortage of that. Lots of local superstitions.'

'You write books, Garry?'

'Yes. Tell me about some of these superstitions.'

'Ah, only stupid people believe all that nonsense about spirits in the bush.'

'I'm not sure if it's nonsense,' Roger mused. 'You remember that incident last year?'

'You mean when you see that ball of fire, Mr Franklin?'

'Yes.'

'Come on now, let's hear the story,' Garry said. 'I'm serious. I'll really work if you spark me off.'

'It still baffles me,' Roger said. 'I've had plenty of time to think about it. One night I was coming in late, riding my horse. I'd just crossed the river . . . it's only a stream, really . . . when I saw a great ball of fire over the trees. In the air, moving. The horse saw it too and shied and almost threw me. It wasn't fatigue, and I hadn't had a drink all day. I suppose I must have imagined it, though I've never convinced myself.'

44

'What was it, then?'

'You tell me. By the time I recovered it had disappeared. I went back to the spot the next day, but there was nothing.'

'Manko say it was a *soucouyant*,' Prekash said. 'But he always talking foolishness.'

'That's the man you want to get hold of,' Roger said. 'He'll give you material for more books than you can write. I wonder if he's around?'

'I seen a light by the cocoa shed when I was coming,' Prekash said. 'He might be there. You want me to go and see?'

'Do you mind?' Garry answered for Roger. 'I'd like to talk with him.'

'You're sure?' Roger asked. 'Not tired?'

'I'm fine.'

Prekash went off, and the two men freshened their drinks. 'Manko is the local obeahman,' Roger explained. 'He works miracles and cast spells.'

'You're not smiling.'

'When you've lived here as long as I have, you grow cautious about what you disbelieve.'

After a short while Rover got up and growled. This time the dog bristled and whined, and Prekash called out from the darkness, 'You better hold Rover, Mr Franklin. He don't like Manko.'

Roger got up and put the dog inside the house. When he turned back Prekash was on the veranda and Manko was sitting at the top of the steps, looking at the drinks on the table. Roger filled a glass and gave him.

'This is Mr Johnson, Manko.'

'Thanks.' Manko acknowledged the drink. He exhibited none of Prekash's nervousness. He spoke to Garry, as if he had been there all the time. 'You wondering why Rover was excited?' Is not that I don't like animals. *They* don't like me.'

Garry looked at the seamed face which appeared to glow. Manko's eyes glistened brightly from the angle of light where he was sitting. Some strange dimension had entered the atmosphere with his coming which puzzled Garry. He was aware of a sudden change of mood, as if he no longer wanted to prolong the evening. The feeling was illogical and he shook his mind and took a sip of his drink.

'So you want to hear about spirits and obeah, eh?' Manko went on. 'Well to start off with, I seen you before.'

'When I arrived?'

'No. It was before you reach to Trinidad.'

Garry quelled a desire to laugh. Roger broke the lengthening pause: 'Come on, Manko. Mr Johnson has never been in Trinidad before.'

'I had a dream.' Manko spoke as if he had the uttermost indifference whether they believed him or not. He quaffed the rum like water and motioned Prekash to fill his glass. Prekash did it without thinking.

Garry was going to speak but Roger waved a silencing hand. He knew Manko's way.

'Seven days after you left England, it had a fire on board the ship.'

Garry did not grasp the significance at once; he said, 'Yes,' and then, keenly, 'how did you know?' His astonishment was directed more to Roger as he turned to him and said, 'I haven't even told *you* that!'

'There was a fire?'

'Yes! It could have been serious if the crew hadn't moved fast.'

'H'mm.' Roger grunted. 'Some sort of mental telepathy?'

'How? Why? It's incredible by any yardstick.'

Before Garry could get over his surprise . . . not untinged with puzzlement . . . Manko went on, 'Also, Mr Johnson, time flying faster for you than anybody else here tonight.'

'What do you mean?' Roger demanded, for even before Garry his thoughts flew to what his friend had said about the critical condition of his old wound.

'Ask Mr Johnson. He don't have many more journeys to make.'

Garry rose and turned his back on them, staring out at the dark hills. The whole tone of the evening had changed so abruptly. Suddenly now he was remembering the girl who had materialized and shocked him and faded away: his emotions now were like they had been then; he felt a connection between the two incidents but could not understand.

46

A rush of recent memories, since he left England, came now, as if in tracing those experiences he would find a link, but all that he could coherently grasp was the transition from one country to the next; as if one minute he had been standing in a London street and the next he was here in this hot island listening to an old man who performed magic.

'Enough of your devilish forecasts, Manko,' Roger said sharply, sensing Garry's disquietude. 'I didn't send for you to put Mr Johnson off. We want entertainment with your stories.'

'That's what he like to do, frighten people,' Prekash put in, feeling left out. 'For my part, I don't believe a word he say.'

'I was talking with Mr Johnson, but he don't answer. Never mind, he and me will have plenty time to talk.' His voice changed. 'Right. Now, what you want to hear?'

'You remember my experience last year, with that ball of fire?' Roger gave a lead as Garry returned to the rocker, still thoughtful, but listening.

'Oh. That was a *soucouyant*. They catch it, though. It was a old woman in the village what used to turn into a *soucouyant* in the night and go to suck human blood. Especially babies.'

'How did she do that?' Garry asked. He wanted Manko to go on talking, so he could have time to think, and study him.

'She used to shed she skin like a snake, and hide it in a mortar. Then she turn into this ball of fire and fly about looking for blood. That same night when she nearly attack Mr Franklin, we went in the hut and rub down the skin with pepper and salt. When she come back, she couldn't put it on. It burn she so much that she start to hop about and scream, "Skin, skin, you don't know me! Skin, skin, you don't know me!"'

Prekash burst out laughing, but felt a fool as the two white men did not share his mirth. In fact, Roger frowned slightly and Garry shot him a disapproving glance. Manko ignored him. In telling the story he had done nothing in the way of emphasis or pantomime to add weight. No gesture or modulation or break in his speech, except that he tried to imitate an old woman's quavering voice as he repeated his last sentence.

It was this lack of demonstration and auxiliary movement that heightened the story.

'Crick, crack, monkey break my back!' Prekash recited the traditional story-teller's ending brightly. 'Wire bend and the story end!'

But it was worse than his laugh: now all three ignored him.

'So what happened, Manko?' Garry asked.

'The people in the village push she inside a barrel and nail it up. Then they roll the barrel in the river. I could have another drink?'

'Sure.' Roger gestured.

'Get it yourself,' Prekash said sulkily.

Garry put the bottle on the floor near to Manko, and he helped himself. He was drinking the rum as if quenching a great thirst and it did not seem to have any effect on him.

'You remember about six-seven years ago, when they shoot a man in the village?' Manko asked Roger.

Roger nodded vaguely.

'That was no man. That was a *lagahoo*. He could change shape and turn into a cow, or a dog, or a donkey, or anything. One night somebody hear a set of heavy chains dragging and rattling in the yard, and what you think he see when he went to look? A black bull. The bull charge him and he grab the chain. The bull turn into a white cow. The man grab the chain harder and the white cow turn into a goat . . .'

'What colour?' Prekash feined interest, but again he got no response.

'It went on so till foreday morning, when the *lagahoo* turn into a cock . . . a red one . . . and fly away. Later on the man had marks all over his body from fighting, so nobody could disbelieve him. That night he borrow a gun and load it with a silver bullet, and when the *lagahoo* come he shoot it dead.'

'You'd better start taking notes,' Roger said facetiously to Garry.

'I wish I were. I'm intrigued enough.' And to Manko, 'I have some questions.'

'I got no answers,' Manko replied promptly, and without

rancour, 'You white people is the ones with brains. You figure it out.'

'Those are all other people's experiences,' Garry said. 'What about yourself?'

'I have too much power for them sort of things to happen to me.'

'You must be a *lagahoo* yourself!' Prekash said, and misfired again.

'When I was a young man like this little boy here, though, before I realize my powers, I went to a dance in the village one night. Suddenly a pretty girl arrive on the scene. When I say pretty, I really mean pretty-pretty. Like a girl we have on the estate, Sarojini.' Manko looked directly at Garry. 'You seen she when you arrive.'

Garry lit a cigarete, but said nothing, though his thoughts were spinning. The image of Sarojini surfaced from his subconscious where he had nestled it for leisurely reverie, but again he could make no connection. It was an odd night . . . if 'odd' was the right word. More like weird. He slapped an imagined mosquito on his cheek to distract Manko's steady gaze.

Manko went on, 'She was the most beautiful girl not only in the dance hall, but that any man had seen in their lives. And the more the other girls get tired dancing, so this one become fresh and lively, prancing up with the men and getting all the women jealous. Well just before midnight she say she had to go, but none of the men would see she home, until I decide to go. We went out and when we was near the bush, pass all the huts, I hear twelve o'clock striking. Same time she ask me for a cigarette. When I light the match, I nearly jump out my skin. The girl face turn old and ugly, with two big eye and a twist-up nose, and all she teeth pushing out of she mouth. I get so frighten I stumble backwards and fall down in a patch of *picker* . . .'

'Thorns,' Roger interrupted for Garry.

'Same time I hear as if a horse stamping. When I look down at the woman foot, I see one of them was a hoof. She start to cackle and laugh, and disappear in the bush. Up to this day I got the marks where the *picker* scratch me.' Manko pulled out his shirt to show them.

'And what was that creature?' Garry asked.

'*La diablesse.* The devil-woman.'

In the pause that followed Roger got up and knocked his pipe out on the parapet. 'Manko will go on all night.'

'At least while the rum last,' Prekash held up the bottle and canted it against the light. There was little left. 'Praise the lord it only got a last drink. You have it, Garry.' He emphasized the name for Manko, trying to regain his self-esteem with a show of familiarity.

'Give it to Manko. I've had enough.'

'Or have it yourself,' Manko told Prekash. 'It might make you grow taller.'

Roger said, as Manko got up, 'Before you two go. I'm giving Mr Johnson complete freedom of the estate, to come and go as he pleases. Let him have anything he wants at any time.'

'Okay Mr Franklin.' Prekash joined Manko on the steps. He thought of lingering and leaving last, to show the obeah-man, that he was there that night as guest and not employee, but thought better of it, remembering how the evening went. The reception given Manko, too, made him brood; the two white men had seemed to accept all the talk of obeah and spirits, when he had expected them to ridicule the old man or at least have a good laugh. There might come a time when he could use Manko, even if he did not believe a word he said himself.

'Maybe you can show him around tomorrow,' Roger told Prekash, 'I'm likely to be very busy for a while.'

'Oh, I'll be all right,' Garry said. 'It'll be much more fun wandering around on my own. I'd rather not plan anything, just take things day by day.'

'That's the best way,' Manko looked at Garry with the merest hint of a smile. 'You and me could have some good talks, Mr Johnson, any time you ready.'

'I'll certainly come to see you,' Garry said.

'When you get a chance. It got a lot to see in Sans Souci, and a lot to do. You might find you don't have as much time as you think.'

'You'd better go now,' Roger said, 'you've given us enough nightmares.'

'Come on Manko.' Prekash started down the steps.

They said good night and went. They cast long shadows in the circle of light, misshapen blobs that reached the darkness of the bush some yards from the house, before they disappeared round the side.

'I'm for bed, and pleasant dreams, I hope.' Roger yawned and turned to go in. 'Coming?'

'I think I'll sit out here awhile.'

'Sure. If you need anything, ring the bell for Eloisa.'

When Roger left he stood gazing out at the night, trying now, in solitude, to reassemble the evening, to use his arrival as a starting point from which to think. He felt as if he had reached the top of a hill but did not want to see what was on the other side. Sarojini intrigued him; Manko had shaken him, and somehow the two experiences were linked, and the old man's uncanny glimpses into the past and future were threads which weaved a pattern about him. But why, and how? Was he foolishly, and quickly, falling under the spell of the tropics, and embroidering casual incidence with mystery and speculation? Manko had done the very same thing with his tales, but with patent deliberation, as if he knew Garry would appreciate his motive. Yet, cluttered with mumbojumbo as they were, he was clear enough when it came to read the past and tell the future. He could not come to any conclusion; by and by, he sat again in the rocker, musing, finding an attraction in his *bafflement*, and he dozed off there thinking about Sarojini.

When Eloisa came to clear away the things she said mosquitoes would kill him *dead* if he slept out here, and he wished her good night and went in.

3

No one can really tell when a settlement becomes a hamlet, a hamlet a village, a village a town, a town a city, a city a metropolis. No one can tell what it is, and when it is that a differentiation is made, nor by whom, nor for why. A man builds a hut in a wilderness of bush and near-jungle . . . perhaps a coalburner, eking out a living by making coal from wood through a sweatful, slow-burning process; there are some such still in Trinidad, in spite of paraffin and calor gas and electricity. A man builds a hut, and lives alone, travelling far for some simple necessity, like a needle, or a sheet of paper. Another man comes and clears a plot and plants corn; he brings a wife and child. Is it now a settlement? By and by they are joined by others: is it now a hamlet? In time there is a shop . . . a mere shed, perhaps, with a rickety counter and a smattering of goods. But it grows. Presently a van makes delivery of such rare and varied items as fresh bread, shirts and buckets. The opening of any estate . . . sugar, cacao, citrus fruit . . . brings people to work and settle. Village now, with perhaps one or two asphalted streets, another shop, and three or four taxis plying on the main road to and from Port of Spain, the City. The drivers would live in a hut and walk barefooted with their latest American models occupying spots in the street like permanent fixtures. Here in this balmy clime there was no need for a garage, and all manner of maintenance and repair were carried out on the selfsame spots. When the cars were no longer serviceable they stayed right there and died, doggedly laying claim to some square feet of the public road. Village now, late laughter in the rumshop, a once-a-year spraying of DDT in the open gutters to decimate the hordes of mosquitoes; gossip and scandal around the stand-pipe where the women filled pitch-oil tins and buckets with water and sometimes squatted, like the children, under the tap for a bath. No one bothers about the originators who first ordained the picturesque names that some of these villages possess ... La Gloria, Flanigin Town, Wilderness, Veronica, Carapichiama, El Dorado and Paradise. The names set in train romantic notions until the eye physically beholds the places they identify. Some are mere stretches of canefield punctuated with an occasional hut; others are so tucked away from the main thoroughfare as to remain forgotten, even unknown. The stray traveller is instantly recognized and his presence denotes only one thing: he is lost, and some bystander would volunteer the direction to the main road.

When Roger revived the cacao estate Sans Souci already claimed the status of village. The inhabitants had depended on the sugar-cane estates which started from their front door and extended for many miles to the south. The cacao estate was behind their huts, moving northwards to the foot of the hills. The village was encircled by a road which started and ended at the main junction. It deteriorated into a bumpy track after a few hundred yards and became a footpath eventually, though wide enough to take single-line traffic, precedence being taken by the first vehicle on. Then, as it circled back to the main road, it resumed the appearance of a proper street. Similarly, the appearance of the village deceived at first with a few houses of concrete with galvanized roofs, thinning out with less imposing dwellings until there was only a small rude shack under a tall cedar tree, open on all sides, a public spot for idling, drinking, and gambling. Near to this, a scant twenty yards away, there grew a giant *pepal* tree which spread clusters of deep-green heart shaped leaves protectively over a Hindu temple. The temple was built under this tree which was worshipped and the yard around its roots was hallowed ground. By night jumbie-birds hooted ominously in its branches where various spirits dwelt, waiting to be evoked by someone in distress. They murmured and whispered in the wind, and villagers shivered to hear the mournful jumbie-birds, for the call portended death and no one knew for whom the bell tolled. The roots of the tree were sprinkled with various coloured liquids, and there were always small brass bowls with offerings for the gods. Sometimes in the dawn village women, shrouded in saris, would kneel before the tree and pray, making wild promises if their wishes were granted. By and by the Pundit would come, riding his bicycle, a large black umbrella strapped to the handle to shelter him from the sun more than the rain, his dhoti rucked up to give his legs freedom for pedalling. The ringing of a bell would summon worshippers . . . mainly women . . . the men would be foraging for the day's bread. If some woman was ill or busy, she sent her daughter. They brought flowers, always they brought flowers, plucked fresh with the sparkle of dew. Some of them had temple duties . . . to prepare for some particular ceremony, or to sweep the yard, or assist the Pundit in his functions. The yard itself was hedged with hibiscus and kept scrupulously clean, swept daily with a *cocoyea* broom . . . one made from the thin stems of the coconut leaf. The yard had been levelled and a mixture of mud and cattle dung . . . the same as used for the walls of huts, and the temple itself . . . formed a smooth, yellowy surface like plaster when it was baked in the sun. The temple had a roof of *carat* leaves, a large fan-shaped palm leaf. It was not as picturesque as in some other villages, with high domes or steeple-shaped facades. It was more utilitarian than fanciful, consisting of a large hall-like room with scattered benches, and a walled-off corner which was the Pundit's domain. The walls were adorned with drawings of Hindu gods . . . primitive work done with ordinary house paint.

During her childhood Sarojini had visited the temple many times, dutifully, but as she grew up she went less frequently. It was not that her faith weakened, but like everyone else she now regarded religion as something separate from day-to-day life, a reposing comfort in time of need, a fountain to freshen waning hope. She lived within sight of the temple, and passed it every day.

But the morning after she saw Garry, her thoughts confused and tinged with excitement, she paused on her way to the stand-pipe. Like countless other mornings dawn was a thing of beauty. With the sun only suggesting the furnace that was to come, early risers had an hour's respite before they literally warmed up to the day's activities. Bluejeans and keskidees, pickoplat and humming bird, semp and cravat, seven-colour parakeets, doves and wood pigeons . . . there was not a variety of birdlife not whirring and flashing in the trees, darting from branch to branch, disporting in an exuberance of play, capturing the morning before it was filled with smoke and movement and noise. Every tree, every hedge and stray vine thrived and blossomed: it was significant that no villager grew flowers, these were bountiful and free. Even the electric wires overhead on tall wooden posts at the side of the road had a kind of parasitic growth, a hardy plant with a tough, serrated leaf that windborn, clung to the wire and thrived, suspended with no visible means of sustenance. A giant samaan tree, with more spread than height, it must have measured three times more across as up, harboured and supported several species of wild vine and orchids along the thick branches and trunk, and even small trees which managed to gain a foothold in the mossy and spongy bark. All these, as if by common consent, flowered in the morning, and there were so many hues and sizes and shapes that only by bulk could the samaan tree itself be identified. The air was sweet and cool, and the blueness of the sky had not yet hardened into the steely blue of another blazing day.

A man passed and nodded to Sarojini as she stood there. He broke a piece of hibiscus and stripped off the bark and chewed the stick to make a frizzly end to clean his teeth. He walked slowly down the road: by the time he got to the stand-pipe, teeth cleaned, he would have a gargle and a wash . . . if those blasted women were not surrounding the pipe and chattering like the flock of seven-colour parakeets in the cedar tree.

Years ago when she was younger the Pundit cast Sarojini's horoscope and foretold an uneventful and prosaic life.

'You mean nothing going to happen to me?'

The Pundit would have liked to forecast something sensational for this pretty child. It seemed impossible that a girl of such rare loveliness would not be involved in some unusual circumstances during her life, in spite of the stars and the planets.

'Look good,' Sarojini said, 'perhaps you miss a sign?'

'Wait a minute,' the Pundit said, 'you might be right you know. Nothing going to happen for a long time . . . five, six years . . . and then, when you near the end of your patience, something BIG will happen.' By that time he thought, if her father Ramdeen hadn't married her off, she would have blossomed into the peak of her beauty, and surely the gods would have designs on her.

During the night Sarojini had remembered what the Pundit said. She was restless and unable to sleep. Several times she regretted her flight from the yard. What stupid thing to do, how he must have laughed. Or perhaps he did not laugh at all, perhaps the brief encounter was like brushing off a mosquito to him. All night she tried to remember what he looked like, but he only came as a blur. Trying to marshal her wild, milling thoughts, she ticked off on her fingers in the dark all the signs that pointed to a crisis in her life. She was about thirteen when the Pundit drew his circle in the dust. She was at the end of her patience. Then there was Manko, divining in some detail a great happiness. And above all, in a warm darkness as she was now, the man slept. Was he thinking of her? She must be mad to feel so, fleeing like some shooed chicken from the yard! Never in her life would she do such a stupid thing again. It seemed now that she was being favoured by the gods, and it was up to her now. Resolved, she had fallen asleep at last, in spite of Ramdeen's drunken snores behind the thin cotton curtain which was all that separated them in the small hut.

Standing by the temple in the dawn, she thought it would not be amiss to make an offering to show her appreciation. She glanced about for flowers and the nearest were hibiscus. She gathered a bunch and went into the temple yard, feeling a little guilty that she had grown negligent, murmuring an apology to the *pepal* tree as she placed the red flowers in an empty brass bowl.

The deed lightened her spirits, and when she met Dummy going for water she rubbed the boy's head playfully and held his eager hand.

Dummy was born deaf and dumb but it was only when he was five years old and needed by his parents to perform odd chores that they realized this. Before that they merely thought he was odd, and the neighbours said there were some children who didn't talk in the beginning, but once they started you would wish they were dumb.

All the children in the village had duties to perform before they went to school on the main road . . . tie the cow or goat out for grazing, sweep the yard, feed the fowls, water the tomato and aubergine plants, fetch water from the standpipe. Dummy suffered a great number of cuffs and clouts for disobedience before the tragedy was discovered and accepted with the resignation of the poor. It did not prevent his being useful, however. Indeed, he soon found that it was only by actions that his existence was acknowledged, and he buzzed about the village like a blue-arse fly, cheerfully working not only for his parents but cunning villagers who took advantage of his handicap. Malnutrition left his first set of teeth permanent. They were small and discoloured, but always on exhibition, for Dummy knew a grin was more welcome than a scowl. It was not the grin of an idiot. He was sharp-witted, and what he lost in his other senses he made up for with a pair of eyes that were bright and keen and filled with a mature reflection, and a pair of hands that magically turned a piece of wood or a scrap of mud into the shape and semblance of everything he beheld.

'You one going to tote that big bucket of water, Dummy?' Sarojini asked as they walked to the standpipe. Everybody spoke to Dummy as if he could hear.

The boy squeezed her hand as if he understood. Of all the women in the village, Sarojini's hands were the softest. Sometimes he wanted to take them and make something, mould the softness into a rainbow, or the sky as it was now at break of dawn, with so much colour he staggered to take it in. As if he heard angels, Dummy's head was always high, searching clouds in the day and counting stars at night.

Only her friend Kamalla was at the standpipe when they got there. Even without the comparison of Sarojini, Kamalla was ugly. They had it to say she paid men to do it with her, and they had to cover her face before they could go into action. Dummy's fingers were ever itching to get themselves on such raw material: he felt he would have done a better job than God. But not with her figure. This was where compensation was paid, in a swell of thigh and breast, and a backside that made music when she walked: another thing the men said, was that she was the most glorious piece if tackled from behind. She was Sarojini's trusted friend, generous, sharp of tongue and full of laughter. She had been to school with Sarojini, and now they both worked on the cacao estate.

'Take off that pants, Dummy,' Kamalla said, 'and let me wash it for you. You worthless vagabond! You been playing in mud again.'

His eyes were constantly on people's lips and gestures and he could read their faces like a book, so it was not difficult to understand them. The pair of short, ragged khaki pants was the only piece of clothing he currently possessed. Dummy never went to school, Dummy never went to parties, Dummy never had to dress up for any reason. Dummy did not cost his parents one single cent in maintenance. It was cheaper to keep Dummy than a goat or a cow or even a stray dog or cat. He ate by caprice, dropping in by any soft-hearted housewife who happened to be near if he was hungry, or he foraged for guavas and mangoes in the bush. In some guilt-ridden fashion everybody in the village felt responsible for Dummy's condition, and made offerings to him as they did to the *pepal* tree. Once they got him chewing on a scrap of roti or a piece of stale bread, or anything whatsoever that was edible and available, they felt they had done their duty. And there was scarcely an hour of day but he received a mouthful of food to keep him alive until the next hour.

The khaki pants, stained with fruit juice and mud, were held up with a piece of rope that would have tethered a ferocious bull. He pulled the pants off, leaving the rope knotted around his waist.

'You know something Sarojini?' Kamalla tittered as he stood naked. 'This boy got to start wearing long pants soon. That *lohlo* getting so big, it will start peeping out!'

Sarojini laughed. Dummy laughed too.

'I keeping an eye on it,' Kamalla said, 'and as soon as he could catch a stand, I will teach him what to do with it!'

Sarojini laughed again, and Dummy tried to say something that came out as a guttural grunt. He experienced a pleasurable excitement standing naked with the two women. He had a sudden urge to pee and held his penis up, sending the piss jetting high across the canal, aiming at a wild pumpkin vine on the other side.

'A-a!' Kamalla exclaimed, exaggerating amazement as she saw it pleased the boy. 'But Dummy, you got a lot of power behind that *lohlo*!'

Dummy's face beamed: he wished he could pee forever.

Kamalla began to scrub the pants under the tap, her knuckles making short shrift of the dirt and mud.

'I ain't got much time this morning, Kamalla. I want to go home quick.'

'We ain't got much work today. Only dancing the cocoa.'

She wrung the trousers and flung them at Dummy. He caught them and put them on, tucking them under the heavy rope belt. In a few minutes they would dry in the heat.

Sarojini filled her bucket. 'I know. But I got a funny feeling something going to happen today. You ever have that feeling?'

'You always saying so from the time I know you.'

'Anyway,' Sarojini began, and left it at that. She was eager to talk to someone, but clutched her feelings preciously. She had waited a long time, she was not going to share with anybody the thrilling emotions that had her body a-tingle. And suppose, just suppose, that nothing came of it in the end, that she was only moving from one dream to another? She stifled the thought stillborn, unable to bear it.

They waited for Dummy to fill his bucket then the three of them set off down the road. Kamalla balanced her bucket on her head, her hands swinging free, the cheeks of her backside quivering like jelly this side and that when she saw a male. Sarojini held hers in one hand, her body slightly tilted the opposite way to compensate, while the other hand clutched her sari, lifting it in that graceful, unconscious posture that the village girls had when carrying a weight in their hands. Dummy walked between them, splashing from a bucket filled to the brim.

Even in that short space of time the morning was beginning to warm up. Kamalla stopped off at the shop to buy fresh hops bread which the van was just delivering, and

Sarojini walked on with Dummy. When the boy got near his hut he ran on the side track that led to it and left his bucket in the yard and came back quickly to rejoin Sarojini. He took the load from her and accompanied her to her hut.

Ramdeen was still asleep. Sarojini prepared breakfast quickly with deft hands, kneading enough flour in a plastic basin to make sufficient roti to take to work for their midday meal. She sat on the step doing this while Dummy made the fire in the earthen fireplace under the small thatched kitchen in the yard. Briskly, she made balls of the dough, then rolled them out in circles on a flat board. She rubbed ghee on them, made a cut from the centre with her fingernail, and rolled them round the circle so they were cone-shaped. She slapped them round again and rolled them back to their original shape. Dummy had the fire going and the *tawah* . . . a flat circle of iron . . . already heating. She slapped a roti on, rubbing it with ghee, and when one side was done she flapped it over and did the other. She clapped the hot roti from the sides when it was done and a puff of steam came out. She put on a pot of *bhagee* . . . a variety of spinach . . . to go with it. Dummy had collected the *bhagee* in the yard . . . it grew untended, like a weed. But it was poor man's food, and when a man was able to hoe it from his yard and plant something else, things were looking up.

Shortly, they were sitting down to breakfast, eating from chipped enamel plates, drinking coco-tea from chipped enamel mugs.

'That damn father of mine, he never get up early,' Sarojini told Dummy. 'He always late for work. Listen to him still snoring inside. Drunk again. God alone know where he get money from to buy rum, and we living so poor, like ants, catch-as-catch-can, and he does be spreeing all over the place as if money does grow on trees.'

She had little love for Ramdeen. Theirs was a strange relationship, with none of the family affiliation which was characteristic of the Indians. Without a mother, she had begun young to take on responsibility, and coping with Ramdeen's indifference and drunkenness had been a struggle until she was old enough to assert herself. Now, he left her alone, but as if begrudging he had to do so, sullen and watchful when they were together, cantankerous and quarrelsome, constantly threatening to bring her to heel. She had grown accustomed to all this and now she paid no attention, grateful that she had escaped from all his threats long enough to become a young woman and control her own affairs. Once she made him realize he could not affect her actions in any way, she found a little room for sympathy, sorry to see him wasting away his life. She was sure the only reason that Mr Franklin kept him on at the estate was because of his long service.

She left Dummy to wash the plates and went into the hut. Under the canvas cot she had an old suitcase in which she kept all her possessions. She took out a blue and gold sari which had belonged to her mother, which she had never worn. She fondled it, strengthening the crazy idea which she had. She could imagine the consternation and remarks if she appeared for work in it. A swift depression came, as if the gods were jealous of her happiness even in speculation. It left her cold, and her heart like lead. Suddenly everything was foolish and senseless and without hope. She wanted to laugh, she wanted to cry, she wanted to go down on her knees and beg forgiveness for entertaining a bigness that was more than she could understand. What presumption and audacity, whom did she think she was, to aim so high, for a target she was incapable of appreciating, swaddled in mystery and mist, merely on the utterings of an old obeahman? A poor village girl, barefoot in the dust, couldn't even speak proper English, never used a knife and a fork, running without reason like a panicked chicken? She should be grateful for small mercies. She should hope for a pair of shoes, or a set of bangles, or some clothes to wear so she wouldn't have to borrow from Kamalla, or just to live another day? She swayed on the cot, burying her head in the sari, shutting her eyes so tight they throbbed. Then as quickly as depression came it went. She laughed aloud, promising herself not to dream too much, to take things one at a time, and squeeze each moment dry before this exhilaration left her. Why shouldn't she wear the blue and gold sari if she wanted? For no reason in particular, really, it would just make a change, it would give them something to talk about on the

61

estate. And she only had to dance the cocoa today, it wasn't dirty work.

Humming, she tucked one end of the sari in her petticoat waistband and spun like a top, wrapping it around her waist. She made several pleats and tucked them in, and flung the loose end over her shoulder. There was nothing but a small handmirror in the hut, she remembered with a frown. Then she thought that Dummy was the best mirror, and she went outside, taking a comb with her.

She watched him with more intensity than he looked at her. She saw puzzlement, then wonder, then joy and admiration. Dummy danced and clapped his hands. He came close and stretched and traced the contours of her body from head to toe, his fingers sliding on the soft silk. He rubbed against her like a kitten, until she had to laugh with delight and push him away.

He combed her hair as she sat on the step, jet-black hair that fell in soft waves below her waist and was iridescent in the first touch of the sun. Usually she made it into a bun or plaited it, today she would let it flow free and blow in the wind.

She sprung up at the long blast of the conchshell from the estate.

'Lord, Dummy, I didn't realize it was so late! I got to take the short-cut.' She had wanted to go and meet Kamalla, but there was no time for that now. Quickly she got the bag with her lunch, shouting out to wake Ramdeen as she left.

Dummy walked with her to the track at the back of the village, which was a shorter but little-used way to the estate.

'You better go back now,' she told him. 'I got to walk fast.'

He fell back and stood watching her go in the distance, the blue and gold sari outstanding in the green bush. He knew it was a happy day for Sarojini, though he didn't know why. Because she was happy, he was happy. He would look for orchids all day to give her when she returned in the evening.

Sarojini's shout came dimly to Ramdeen and he stirred. He opened his eyes and stared at the thatched roof for a long time, recalling his thoughts which of late were taking more and more time to come back. Where did they go when they left a man in sleep? Did they roost in the *pepal* tree with the jumbie birds and the spirits? He groaned and jerked his head to discard the idea. The blasted thing was, when they came back, they came with all sorts of confusing notions, as if they wanted to baffle a man even before he started the day. *Pepal* tree my arse, he thought, and the abuse bolstered his energy enough for him to stretch and fumble for cigarettes and matches on the floor. A man could not divine the first thoughts he would wake with in the morning. When they came back from their nocturnal ramblings in the *pepal,* there had to be some in front and some behind, and strangers in their midst. He wished the whole blasted set of them would just stay there and leave him alone, instead of coming to give him a headache even before he washed his face.

The first person to come to mind was Sarojini and that put him in a bad mood right away. It started a train of thought backwards to the wish that she had never been born. What a time that was, with Kayshee dying in the hut and only Manko and Mr Franklin there to help him. It had seemed the best thing to send for the estate owner, but even though he was white he wasn't able to do anything for her, and afterwards he turned like a hurricane on Ramdeen and wanted to know why he hadn't been informed before, and why Ramdeen hadn't arranged for a midwife. Ramdeen stayed outside under the tonca-bean tree, nursing his pride with a bottle of rum while Mr Franklin and Manko were in the hut. Even the thin weak wail as the child was born failed to stir him. And then he felt like burning down the hut when it didn't turn out to be a boy-child. At least Kayshee could have left him with a boy before she died, so he could face his friends with some dignity, instead of a wailing, wrinkled girl who would cause trouble and botheration and give him grey hairs before his time. It was only when she was old enough to tote water from the stand-pipe and make herself generally useful that he paid any attention to her. It struck him that she was becoming more and more like her mother, and the villagers noticed it too. 'Sarojini really take after she mother, she don't have Ramdeen features at all!'

What the hell did he care? He was just anxious to take her away from the school on the main road and put her out to work. Perhaps he would get her married off early, she was the prettiest girl in the village, and already he had had offers. There was that boy Prekash . . . his parents were offering three cows. He asked Mr Franklin what he should do and was surprised how strongly the estate owner advised him against it, saying that he did not agree with child-marriages, and that there was a job waiting for Sarojini on the estate. But all the same Ramdeen was tempted to get rid of her. He got a deposit of ten dollars from Prekash's parents, and the rumour went around that Sarojini was going to be a bride. It was a rumour that was to last for many years, for Sarojini turned out to be a goose laying a golden egg (Ramdeen like to think in parables and proverbs) and Ramdeen secretly vowed she would marry over his dead body. The miracle of good fortune came one morning from a visitor who said he was a Welfare Officer touring the district. In his usual state of drunkenness, Ramdeen paid scant attention to what the man was saying. And he was talking a lot, some foolishness about terms and conditions, and woes and poverty. It was a hot morning; they were standing in the yard and as the voice droned on like a bee Ramdeen suddenly broke in.

'I don't want to hear no more stupidness. Go.'

The man was surprised. 'You turning away good money?'

'What money?'

'Man Mr Ramdeen, I just been through the whole business, explaining it to you. Twenty dollars a month. At the post office on the main road. Waiting for you to collect.'

'For me?' Ramdeen rubbed his face. He wished things didn't happen before he came to grips with the day. Only after a few drinks would he begin to tick.

'Yes. That's if she don't married, of course. If that happen, the money cut off right away.'

'If who don't married?'

The man sighed. 'I just tell you. Your daughter.'

'Sarojini?'

'Yes.'

'If Sarojini don't married, I get twenty dollars in the post office?'

'That's what I been trying to explain all this time. Every month.'

'A *fresh* twenty dollars every month?'

'Yes.'

'You must be making joke!' It wasn't only his thoughts now; he was beginning to see and hear things.

The man said, going, 'It start today. You could go and collect the first twenty now.'

When the visitor left Ramdeen sat down under the tonca-bean for a long time, wondering if the rum had made him crack in the head at last. It was a good dream, though. A man didn't dream about twenty dollars every day. It was a pity it couldn't be real.

The next day the postman passing on his bicycle stopped by the hut and tinkled his bell until at last Ramdeen came out.

'What the arse you want?'

'They got something for you in the post office, Ramdeen,' he said, and rode off.

Ramdeen decided to report the postman for creating a disturbance and dropped in at the post office, seeing as it wasn't such a long walk in the hot sun.

'You don't want your money, or what?' The Chinese-creole girl behind the counter scowled at him.

It was a great conspiracy, and the proof of the pudding was in the eating.

'All right,' he conceded. 'Let me see it and feel it, and spend it, and then I would believe.'

'First you got to sign here.'

'Ah!'

'You can't sign? Make your mark, then, or your finger-print.'

Ramdeen made his fingerprint to see how far the joke would go.

It was only when he tendered one of the bills in the shop for a bottle, and had a drink, that the miracle came to him. Another man might have been intrigued to ponder the whys and wherefores, and carry but a single hibiscus or frangi-pani to the temple yard and offer it to the *pepal* tree for this windfall from the blue. But Ramdeen did not look the gift

65

horse in the mouth. With his third drink he made the vow that Sarojini would die a spinster, that monkey would smoke Prekash's pipe as far as the marriage was concerned, unless he went to the post office after a month and found that he was not the 'Mr Ramdeen' who should have received the money. But he was the Mr Ramdeen all right, as he found out month after month since that day. He made all sorts of excuses when Prekash pressed his suit, not wanting to put him completely off, holding his potential as a husband in reserve. You could never tell what might happen, and Prekash was working for big money. Overseer of Sans Souci, h'mm!

Early that morning Manko rolled the roofs of the cocoasheds away, exposing the beans to the sunlight. They were strewn in their thousands on a wide expanse of platform. The roofs, large inverted V-shaped coverings of corrugated galvanize, were divided evenly in two over each platform, the halves moving apart on small iron wheels along tracks at the sides of the platforms. One man could do this job, and it was necessary in case of a sudden downpour of rain, when they were swiftly rolled back into position. Rain was the worst enemy of people who had cocoa drying in the the sun. The sheds were elevated about five or six feet off the ground.

The woman were dancing the cocoa . . . turning the pods to dry evenly with their feet, a shuffling, dragging movement not without grace.

Every now and then Kamalla paused and looked at Sarojini. The amazement and exclamation which had greeted Sarojini in her sari was going to be the topic of the day for all day unless something even more dramatic happened. If not Kamalla, then one of the other women would stop and shake her head and make a remark about the sari or her hairdo. The remarks were neither adverse nor complimentary. It was sanity that was in question here. But nothing could dampen Sarojini's high spirits. When Prekash saw her he was stunned speechless. Perhaps he might have aided his cause if he had shown some admiration or approval. Instead, he burst out, after staring:

66

'What sort of Carnival going on here today at all? You come to work or you come to play mask?'

'I wear what I like, when I like, how I like.' Her voice was cool. Wrapped in that sari she felt nobody could touch her. 'The day ain't come yet when you, nor no man, could tell me what to wear.'

'You must be crazy. People come on the estate to work. Look at the other women, they dress for it. Even the men have on khaki pants. I could wear pretty clothes too if I want.' Prekash glared with anger.

'Please yourself. Only, it won't make no difference what you put on.'

That set the women laughing at him, and they egged her on 'Tell him, Sarojini, tell him!'

'I got nothing to tell him,' Sarojini said, and got ready to dance the cocoa.

'In any case, you only displaying your ignorance coming to work dress like that.' He tried to hold their attention, but they all ignored him. 'Listen all of you.' He had to talk loud; he tried to put authority in his tone. 'Mr Franklin got a guest, Mr Johnson.' He continued as if he were giving personal orders and not passing on Roger's instructions. 'I want you all to treat this man like you treat Mr Franklin himself. Let him have anything he want, and if he give any orders, obey them. I don't want no disrespect.'

The women murmured. Kamalla said, 'When you say let him have anything he want, you mean *anything*?'

'You know damn well what I mean, Kamalla! Show him that you got good manners before he think the whole set of you just ignorant and backward. These people from England have some funny ideas when they come here. They think we live like cannibals in Africa.'

'It only got one boss around here as far as I concern,' Kamalla said, 'and that is Mr Franklin. I do what he tell me to do.'

'Well is Mr Franklin who say to tell you all.' Always, he had to back down when he tried to make a stand. But one day. 'Anybody step out of line, and bam!' He gestured there would be trouble.

Sarojini had moved away from the others, trying to still

the pounding of her heart only at the mention of his name. She was jealous of this public announcement, as if she had to share him with the others.

Prekash went away to saddle a horse to go down into the cacao. He was in a nasty mood, troubled with a foreboding of misfortune, as if nothing was going to turn out in his favour, and he was helpless to turn the tide. He wished he had a hundred ears and eyes, for it was a large estate and he couldn't be in two places at one time. Unless he turned obeahman like Manko. Thought of the old man recalled the night before and only made him feel worse. When he got the horse he spurred it savagely into the cacao.

The thin cotton curtains were only a transparent barrier to the flood of golden light that streamed through the window. It made Garry think it was late when he awoke, but his watch said it was only six o'clock. He tried to fall off to sleep again, but gave up and lay on the white cotton sheets, allowing his thoughts to come slowly. Two mosquitoes had succeeded in getting through the net and were suspended on it now, their bodies swollen with his blood. Outside the house he could hear the chatter of birds and other small sounds he did not bother to define. He luxuriated in the knowledge that he had nothing particular to do. There was no compulsion to involve himself in the day. He reflected on the things that had happened to him, but with no great concentration. Not that the new day wiped out anything, but he felt like casting himself adrift and allowing events and circumstances to determine his actions and thoughts.

After a while he sneaked up on the two mosquitoes which were close to each other and clapped them dead: the two stains of blood merged on the new net. No doubt Eloisa would have something to say about that. He got up and showered and dressed, white shirt and shorts, and went downstairs.

There was a short note from Roger on the dining table: 'Do what you like when you like. When I'm here, I'll be in the office.'

He sat down and Eloisa came from the kitchen with the halves of a freshly-picked grapefruit.

'Morning Eloisa.'

'Breakfast time is seven o'clock.'

'You should have given me a call.'

'Being as is your first morning Mr Roger say to let you sleep late.' Roger had actually said to let him get up whenever he pleased. 'But don't worry, I will call you in future.'

'Late? It's only eight o'clock!'

'People get up here crack o' dawn.'

'I never get up before nine o'clock in London.' He sprinkled brown sugar on the grapefruit. 'You don't have to bother specially for me, Eloisa.'

'What you want for breakfast?'

'Whatever you've got. I don't eat much in the morning.'

She went into the kitchen. By the time he was through with the grapefruit she had placed a number of dishes on the table. Sliced avacado sprinkled with a little salt and freshly ground black pepper, and oil; fried eggs; sardines garnished with onions and tomatoes; a bowl of *buljol* which he afterwards found out was made of roasted, salted cod; toast and butter and guava jam: a jug of cocoa, and a wooden platter laden with oranges, mangoes, pawpaws and some other fruit unknown to him.

Garry looked at her. 'I told you not to bother!'

'Not no bother. This is just ordinary breakfast.'

'All this? I don't know how to begin.'

'You got to keep up your strength in this hot sun. Mr Roger say you need fattening up.'

'There's enough here for a regiment.'

'Regiment?'

'An army.'

'You just eat up your breakfast like a good boy now. You not in London now. This is Sans Souci.'

Garry surveyed the spread and shook his head as she left him to it. When he began he found that he had a good appetite, but it was impossible to make much inroad in such a feast. Once he looked up and saw her peeping at him from the kitchen, and made a valiant attempt to take another mouthful.

When she came to clear the things he said, truthfully, 'That's the greatest breakfast I've ever had.' He saw that she was pleased, and went on, 'You'll spoil me before I leave.'

'You best hads put on a hat, Mr Johnson, if you going out in that hot-sun.'

'I haven't got one.'

'Mr Roger got two. You best hads wear it even if it don't fit, before you get sun-stroke.' Her eyes roamed on his white skin and she sniffed. White skin meant only sickness to her. Between the hot sun and herself, she would have him a nice, brown healthly look before he went back to England.

Roger's cork hat didn't fit him and he left it behind, making sure Eloisa wasn't looking. He would have to get one . . . sun glasses too, he thought as he winced and blinked. shading his eyes with his hands as he got outside.

It was pleasant to think he could turn in any direction. He saw figures moving by the drying sheds and moved off slowly : Roger had warned him about moving fast in the heat, advising him to take it easy as the slightest effort would leave him sweating. Even so, before he had covered the distance tiny streams of sweat coursed down from his armpits, and he was wiping his face.

As he approached he could see the women working. He did not make out Sarojini but the startling blue of the sari drew his eyes.

It happened they were on a downward sweep and their backs were turned when he came up, and none of them noticed his presence. But he recognized her now: it could be nobody else. Suddenly an elation came over him, as if the day was just born, as if nothing had happened since that fleeting glance yesterday and this moment now. He lost the calm with which he had fronted the day, coming to life with a surge of emotion he had never experienced. He was confused; she was going further away from him and he shouted: 'Sarojini!'

Her stride broke. She did not have to look back to see who it was. They were near the far end of the platform and when they got there she was going to jump off and run and run far into the cacao and hide behind the wings of an immortelle root.

70

'Sarojini!'

She started and shook. Kamalla said, 'As if I hear you name call, Sarojini,' and they turned, dancing, for the upward sweep.

She kept her head low, tugging the sari over it. She whispered fiercely to herself. 'Don't run like a fowl! You dress up for him, and now he standing up right there waiting for you. If you don't make the most of it, you will never get a chance again!'

Kamalla said, 'Oh God, it look like the new white man!'

Perhaps if she looked up now and saw him from a distance, it would be easier when they got close. And in any case, why was she so nervous? Because he knew her name? There was nothing special about it. Don't expect anything, and nothing will happen. Just be your natural self.

She lifted her head, the sari falling on her shoulders, and he saw her coming. The dance was slow, she moved as in a dream, etched in golden light, and the gold threads of the sari shimmered with her movement.

He stood there waiting, and he heard Kamalla say, 'Answer the mister, Sarojini!' The other women looked away, abashed at the presence of the white stranger, *too* glad he had singled out Sarojini to be the embarrassed one.

She looked at him but did not see him, and they turned again, churning the beans. The sound of the tumbling seed was like spent waves shuffling on a sandy beach.

He said: 'Good morning, Sarojini.'

She turned and stood there, scuffing at the pods. One hand had made a desperate clutch to retain Kamalla for company but she had jerked away.

'What are you doing?' he asked softly.

'Dancing the cocoa.'

'That's a nice phrase. What for?'

'So it could dry in the sun.'

'It looks great fun. Can I try?'

'Men doesn't dance cocoa. Only women.'

'Well. I want to, anyway.'

He climbed the steps to the platform and stood close to her. She fled far away: she was surprised to find she could only sway.

'Will you show me how?'

'You shouldn't stand up on the beans with shoes on,' she told his feet.

'I'll take them off.' He sat on the edge of the platform and unlaced his shoes.

'Like this?' Garry twiddled his toes in the pods.

'Yes,' she told his feet.

'Come on then. Let's catch up with the others. You ought to have a partner when you're dancing.'

He held her hand and felt a tremor run through her. For a moment it was like touching a piece of wood, lifeless, then she relaxed as they moved off.

Further down the platform, Kamalla glanced behind and exclaimed, 'Oh God! Sarojini dancing with the white man!'

'What!'

'Yes! She holding hands, and they coming down here! Let we sing a song and give them music!'

Kamalla started to hum an Indian air which they sometimes sang to break the up and down monotony of the dance. The others joined in as they turned, eager to see the sight for themselves.

Garry directed Sarojini so as to pass them at the side. Her head was low: she was still looking at his feet, afraid to let them see her face. They stifled peals of laughter, tittering and pointing to Garry's white feet, already stained brown by the cocoa pods. Garry looked at them and winked. As they saw his mirth, and realized he was enjoying the situation too, they could contain themselves no longer. They openly expressed their delight, breaking step, two of the older ones sat down on the beans and wiped their eyes with the ends of their saris, and Kamalla made some rude remark which provoked fresh peals. Even Sarojini smiled now, her mind growing easier with their participation, and Garry left her and struck out on his own in a shuffling tango, deliberately funny, and they clapped and made carefree laughter.

No one heard Prekash ride up. He stood in the stirrups taking in the scene. His shout was a mixture of anger and uncertainty.

'What going on here?'

72

They fell silent. Sarojini rejoined the other women and they moved away from Garry.

'Come on Prekash,' Garry called gaily, 'tickle your toes!'

'I got work to do, Mr . . . Garry.' He turned to the women. 'You all should know better than to behave so disgraceful. If I don't report the whole set of you to Mr Franklin, my name not Prekash.'

'They're not to blame at all.' Garry moved towards Prekash, concerned. 'It was all my fault, Prekash. They were working hard and I interrupted them.'

'They should of been on another platform by now. This cocoa got to dry quick, Garry, before the rainy season start up'.

'Yes. Well, I'll let them get on with it. I'm really sorry for disrupting things.' Garry sat down and put on his shoes.

'I just going over to the west side,' Prekash said. 'You want to come with me and see some of the estate? I could saddle a horse for you.' He did not like the idea of Garry being with the women, especially Sarojini. Manko spoke a lot of foolishness, but there was no sense in pushing them together.

'I think I'll just amble about on my own this morning.'

'Please yourself.' He was sorry now he had said he was going in the cacao. He wanted to hang about and keep an eye on things. At the same time, he did not want to appear as if he was keeping Garry under observation. He flung a final warning to the women as he rode off: 'If you all don't dance all the cocoa today, I going to dock your pay. Especially you, Miss Sarojini.'

She hated him for sneaking up like a spy. Unwittingly, he gave her the courage she needed to speak.

'Don't bother with Prekash, Mr Johnson. He only jealous.'

'Jealous?'

'He got an idea that I frighten of him, but I don't belong to no man. He was only trying to show off. Everybody know what he like.'

'It was silly of me, anyway.' He called out to the others: 'I'll talk to Mr Franklin, don't worry about your pay.' It was time to go, yet he lingered. 'You're here every day?'

'Yes.'

'I say you yesterday, when I came.'

'I see you too.'

They were both awkward, avoiding each other's eyes.

'Well,' he said, 'thanks for the set.'

'Set?'

'The dance. Haven't you ever been to a dancehall?'

'No.'

'Well.' He thought of something to say. 'Prekash was displeased.'

'He forget it take two hand to clap.'

He looked up at the hills. 'What's over there?'

'A lot of bush and bamboo. And the river. Some cacao too.'

'Is there a road?'

'It got a track, but it hard to find.'

'I hope I don't get lost.'

'I don't see any of the men around, else you could of got one of them to go with you.'

'I'll be all right.' He turned to go.

'Wait.' She could only think that if he went now, she might never see him, or be with him, like this again. 'I know over there well.' She took a deep breath. 'Maybe if I come a little way . . .'

'Will you?' He asked eagerly as she hesitated.

'Kamalla and the others could finish the dancing. And besides, Prekash self say that Mr Franklin say to obey you.'

'You won't get in any trouble?'

She came down from the platform quickly, before fear could overcome her boldness, and started to walk across the yard without looking to see if he followed. Garry caught up with her and they walked off into the bushes side by side, but in silence.

Kamalla watched them until they disappeared. 'Bang-a-lang-a-lang!' She cried, jumping up and down on the platform, crushing and bruising the pods, 'Sarojini create sensation in Sans Souci today!'

They quit work. A hubbub of opinion and excitement filled the air. When would such an event take place again.

After a time the track grew narrow and overgrown with small bushes, and Garry had to walk behind her. All this time they were silent: he would not have known what to

74

say. There were little sounds about them that he only half heard; strange trees and flowers, and birds in every branch, that he was aware of but could not focus in his confused state. He knew only an exhilaration that was tinged with fear and wonder. It was as if something was happening to him over which he had no control.

It was partly like that with her too, only she was much stronger now. She was glad that he did not speak. What was the use of talking? There would be plenty of time for that. She was calm as if everything had been resolved. There was no surprise that he was here with her. She knew exactly where she was taking him. One day Dummy had urged her to follow him to a spot she knew near the river. She thought he wanted to show her a nesting bird or a new flower he had discovered: there seemed little else, as they were surrounded by bush on either hand and the trees grew thick. Here, in fact, the track disappeared completely under an overhanging thorny shrub that made passage irksome. But Dummy led her off the track and up a slight incline, parting the branches of the small trees which snapped back to form a green screen behind them. When they got to the top of the hillock she gasped with surprise. Here the river meandered over rocks to make a small waterfall. Here there were orange and tangerine and grapefruit trees, clustered about an immortelle so high she couldn't see the top. The citrus were old and covered with moss, as if forgotten. There was grass at the foot of the immortelle. . . the only spot, as far as she knew, that it grew on the estate. It seemed a haven for birds and butterflies. She had never known of its existence, and doubted if anybody but Dummy knew, because there was a horseshoe of thick foliage hiding it from the track. Only by coming from the direction of the hills and braving a long stretch of tangly jungle was it accessible . . . and nobody ever came that way. It was a beautiful spot, and she remembered it and led Garry to it.

They had been walking for half an hour, but the overhead trees had shaded them from the sun. Here, it filtered through the leaves, with patches of blue sky and cloud.

Still there were no words. She put her hand on his arm and they stood quiet: he felt she wanted him to see this hidden, wild garden for a minute, with the world behind them.

Without looking at him Sarojini loosened her sari and slowly went down on the grass, as if haste would desecrate the spot and the moment. And as slowly he laid beside her and took her in his arms. He felt everything but lust, and as he fondled her gently she too responded with slow measure, not shy or reluctant, but as if it would be unseemly to hurry, as if the quick surrender must be stretched out in time to cover all the words they had not spoken, all the things they had not done before to get to know each other and lead up to such a moment. It was as if they both knew there would be another time, after the essential union was accomplished, for them to go backwards and pleasure in coming together as for the first time. End first, and begin after.

She only said, at one stage, and it was only a whisper, and entirely unnecessary, 'Don't hurry.'

4

Roger did not need Manko to forecast that in the following weeks he would be spending most of his time away from Sans Souci. The controversy over using cacao land to expand the sugar industry was a matter in which he was bound to be involved. There was only the main road, south of the estate, and a narrow strip of vegetable cultivation, and the built-up areas which separated cacao from sugar-cane; the latter dominating the central plains and driving the other crop into the hills and the virgin forests. While Roger, and one or two other big estate owners, were not worried, the smaller planters were likely to suffer from any decision in favour of sugar. 'If we don't make a stand, not one cacao tree would be left in the island,' one of them told him. Roger could hardly refuse when he was asked to join a small committee quickly formed to consider the matter. He was wary of all committees and sub-committees. Experience had taught him that too much time was wasted in bickering and argument, in absenteeism at important meetings, and a general attitude of siesta and procrastination. Then someone motivated by the boredom and inaction would suddenly come to life and propose some drastic measure to which they would all appear to agree. But it would only be because they wanted to shorten the meeting . . . everyone was busy, everyone had something urgent to attend to . . . for afterwards they would pair off and argue at great length, as if the formal proceedings of the meeting itself had tied their tongues. At the last meeting it had been tentatively agreed to stage a demonstration in Woodford Square. Roger was not sure if this would further their cause, nor if he was prepared to give his men time off to march around the city toting placards in the hot sun. They were busy picking and drying cocoa to bag and send out before the rainy season.

His doubts were shared by Devertie, one of the seven-man committee, an old, aristocratic planter whose French-creole forebears had raised cacao in the Maracas Valley since the first generation. Roger had met him a few times in the early days, and they had a mutual respect for each other. It was at his house in Maracas, a splendid building atop a hill, that the meetings were held.

As the others drove off after this one, Devertie asked Roger to stay for a drink. They sat in large wicker chairs on the south side. His host waved at the view. From this height the plains of Caroni, the island's chief sugar area, could be seen rolling away from green to misty blue until the San Fernando hill . . . the only elevation for some thirty miles.

'I grow cacao,' Devertie smiled, speaking in a college-educated voice, 'and I look at cane all day.' He sighed, an old man with a large family he sometimes lost track of . . . two sons in England, a daughter at the University of the West Indies in St Augustine, another living in Grenada, married to a prosperous cacao grower, and a third who had disappeared into the social backwaters of Port of Spain. He walked with a stick, his joints rheumatic from the damp of the valley.

'You see how it is,' he went on after a pause, 'we should have had three men on the committee for the most. Seven too much. What you think about this demonstration?'

Roger told him.

'Me too. I think we should send a delegation to Trinidad House and let the Government know how we feel, instead of all that marching.'

'Or have discussions with the cane farmers. I'm all for settling things out of court. This business could go on for years.'

'You right. Good crop this year. How about you?'

'Looks good, if we can finish before the rain.'

'You know what these fellars are going to say.' Devertie had a habit of speaking disjointedly, without pause, moving back and forth like a humming bird testing blooms for the sweetest nectar: one had to listen carefully to connect. 'They going to say that is all well and good for you and me, being the largest estates, but,' and he implied the rest with a wave of his hand.

'I just hate the long, drawn-out process, though things might be all right in the end.'

'Cane does grow anywhere, you know. These days they inventing all kinds of harvest machines what could climb hills.' Devertie had this nightmare of cane overrunning every acre of land in the island, high or low: he wanted to leave something for his sons when they returned from England.

'Don't lose perspective,' Roger said.

'We must visit socially,' Devertie said. 'We don't see each other until something like this happen.'

'I don't go out much, since my wife died.'

'That was years ago. You don't have friends in Port of Spain?'

'A few.'

'You never had any children?'

'No.'

'Have another drink.' Devertie had brought out whisky especially for Roger. 'I got a large family, Franklin. So much that I don't even know who gone where or what or why. I thought they would comfort me in my old age. You see that range of hills over there?' He pointed east, and Roger nodded without looking. 'That's all that separate Sans Souci from the Maracas Valley. If we plant cacao on the hills, we join up. You ever thought of that?'

'No.'

'It worth thinking about, you know.' His voice grew serious, but it was still possessed, with very slight inflexion, as if he had all the time in the world, undisturbed. 'If you and me join forces, we control the situation completely.'

'You think so?'

'Sure. The two biggest estates, what you expect?' Devertie sat upright with his stick in front of him, his hands resting on the knob so they were slightly higher than his head, as if he were about to get up any moment.

Roger liked this gentle man, so full of dignity, and respect for other people. The French creole stock were a proud breed: it was a pity so few of them remained. He knew Devertie had no need to seek a liaison with him: the careless suggestion was meant more as a gesture of friendliness than anything else, with no ulterior motive.

Home that evening, he said to Garry, 'Good lord, we're well into a new month. What's happened to the time? But I warned you.'

'I've been all right.'

'I ought to organize something. A bridge party. A trip to one of the beaches. You haven't been anywhere.'

'I don't know about you, but I'm not complaining. I've been collecting material for the book. I'm hooked on it now.'

'Well, you look much better,' Roger admitted. Garry had passed the stage of peeling skin and bumps from insect bites, and there was a sparkle in his eye.

'As long as you're happy. We ought to go some place soon, though. Balandra Bay isn't far from here. A good beach.'

But when Garry went, it was with Sarojini. From an ending, they moved together in such concert that it never seemed strange that they had no beginning. And he did not want to find it. He did not want to stop and say: Well now, how did this start, and why, and if. There was a sensational jumble of time and place and incident in his mind: the sun; the towering red-crowned immortelle; the perfume of ripe golden oranges; the sound of the wind and the river. And Sarojini. Whatever made him happy, whatever eased his heart, whatever stilled doubt and rested him. Her innocence infected him not like a raging fever, but like how sometimes one welcomes a small illness which takes the edge from care and worry. She offered a respite from the cynicism and apathy that followed so quickly the heels of experience and age. He felt he needed a new dimension in language to communicate the simple, pristine quality of the love she brought him. He had tried to say *I love you* and was overcome by a foolish embarrassment, as if sentiment had hardened and petrified inside him. Touch of lip, touch of hand, touch of body to make a oneness with her, purging and purifying him to make him like a child again; not *re*discovering but discovering a butterfly resting on a flower, a certain motion of leaf in wind, a particular note of purling water. Sometimes they loved tenderly and sometimes they were like animals in the grass.

But always it was good. Tangerines ripened and fell; young cacao matured from shining purple to a deep crimson and brown which would become yellow-green for harvest; the very grass they lay on withered for the rainy season. Passage of time was assiduously avoided, because it would make them look for a beginning. To locate themselves in time would bring attendant questions that would want answers, it would call for shape and pattern and limitation and destruction.

So the days went. He never questioned her freedom to leave the compound. Each day she showed him places they could meet unseen, where she had rambled with Dummy. She had an amazing knowledge of Sans Souci and its environs, and knew all the old villagers who supplied him with information for his book.

It was Sarojini who suggested the beach. They had met in the afternoon and made love, and afterwards stripped naked and splashed in a shallow, cooling pool of the river. Drying on the warm rocks, she said, 'I never had a sea-bath.'

'Really?'

'No. I never even see the sea.' She laughed. 'And yet it so near. Sometimes they give a bus excursion in the village, but I never went yet.'

'Not even Balandra Bay?'

'Oh, you know!' She was pleased. 'Mr Franklin told you? We must go one day. As long as it not Good Friday!'

He teased her with silence, knowing she wanted him to ask what was wrong with Good Friday.

'Because,' she said now, 'is bad luck to bathe in the sea on Good Friday. You will turn into a fish. Make some notes for the book. And another thing, before I forget. You break a egg in the sun when is midday, and it will tell your fortune.'

'We don't have to do that when we have Manko. We must go to see him soon.'

'I rather go by the sea. Tomorrow?'

'Could we walk there?'

'In that hot-sun! Is a long walk. I think. We could catch a taxi on the main road.'

It was the first time they would be going out of Sans Souci, and she wasn't sure it was such a good idea to move out of the familiar surroundings of the estate and the village, which seemed so much to enhance the security of their love. But Garry was enthusiastic.

She thought she would prepare a meal for them to eat on the beach, and went early in the morning to see if she could wheedle a chicken from Kamalla, and borrow a sari. Clothes were beginning to become important, and the damp thought of her poverty, which always lurked at the back of her mind, was becoming irksome. It was a good thing that Kamalla was her friend.

'Aha!' Kamalla greeted her, 'What this stranger doing in my yard?'

'What stranger?'

'Well, it look as if you give up your job. And not only that. I forget I ever know you.'

'You self, Kamalla! My best friend!'

'I maybe uses to be your best friend, but not now. You take off like a kite, flying high, nobody could touch you!'

'I just come to borrow a chicken and a sari. I will pay you for the chicken when I get pay.'

'Pay? It don't look like you working any more, Sarojini. You are a lady of leisure,'

'Do quick. I ain't have much time.'

But Kamalla intended to satisfy her curiosity. Not that it was any mystery . . . everybody knew what was happening, or suspected, but rumours were too bare, she wanted a blow-by-blow account from the horse's mouth, and the horse was here now, under an obligation. It was an opportunity not to be missed. But there was a way to go about it. By implication and gesture, intonation and cadence, which would give new meanings to old words; shifting of stance, roll or sparkle of eye, downcast head or raised eyebrows . . . all the plays of pantomime had to be put to use.

KAMALLA: What you want chicken for, pray?

SAROJINI: To eat. What else?

KAMALLA: He like chicken?

SAROJINI: You ever been by the sea?

KAMALLA: No. You?

SAROJINI: I going today.

KAMALLA: You tired of doing it in the bush?

SAROJINI: A young chicken that would cook quick.

KAMALLA: It nice in the water, girl. Only thing, you got to stand up to do it. Oysters is what you want to strengthen him with.

SAROJINI: Who?

KAM'ALLA: I hear you feeling poorly these days, that's why you missing work.

SAROJINI: Yes.

KAMALLA: Funny thing, though. Some people, when they sick, they look even better than when they well! Your cheeks all rosy and red, and your eyes like stars.

SAROJINI: It must be the fever.

KAMALLA: Couldn't be anything else! Couldn't be no stupid thing like a man could cause that! Aye, I nearly forget, girl, it have rumours about Sans Souci that Mr Franklin visitor writing a book!

SAROJINI: In truth?

KAMALLA: Yes. I mean, he got to keep himself occupied, not so? Sans Souci not no tourist resort. But the joke is, he always getting lost. I would of apply to be his guide, but I hear he got one already.

SAROJINI: Who?

KAM'ALLA: People really malicious. They say this girl-guide only guiding him in one direction. You ever seen them together?

SAROJINI: No, you?

KAMALLA: No. I wonder what they does do all day? But Prekash wonder most of all. You should see him riding about all over the estate like a blue-arse fly, trying to catch them. He always asking for you. I tried tell him that you not feeling well these days.

SAROJINI: This fever hit me bad.

KAMALLA: I could see that! Best hads be careful, eh. You taking anything for it?

SAROJINI: The best medicine in the world.

KAMALLA: H'mm, some medicine don't agree with people. Careful lest you take a overdose.

It went on like that for some time, with innuendo and interjection, thrust and parry, as Kamalla got the chicken and the sari.

Sarojini locked the wings of the chicken, and held it

83

dangling by the feet. When she got home she held the head and swung it around briskly a few times, popping the neck. She left it jerking and convulsing on the ground while she boiled water to pour over it to make the plucking easier. She would make a curry chicken, dry and spicy. As she worked she thought about her conversation with Kamalla, but did not allow it to encroach on her mood. Some time in the dance there would have to be a pause and she would have to open her eyes, but that was dim and far away, a vague threat hovering in the background which she ignored in the vibrant, living hours of her love.

When she was going to the main road to meet Garry, she saw Dummy. On a sudden impulse she decided to take him with them: his presence would help to alleviate any strangeness she might feel on this first trip out of the village, and he would be no bother; Garry had already made friends with him. They had met him hunting birds or chasing squirrels in the cacao, and if anything, it had bound them even closer in a warmness and sympathy for the boy.

As long as he was with them, Dummy did not care where they were going. When he got over the thrill of being in a taxi . . . they had given him the end seat . . . he stroked Garry's arm and pressed up close, comparing it with his own.

But it was when they got to Balandra Bay . . . about half an hour's drive . . . that he went crazy with delight. It amused them to watch his antics as he romped on the sand and stared disbelievingly at the sea for long spells, and dashed up to where they sat under a sea-almond tree, creating the shape of the ocean with his hands, eyes bursting with eloquence. Sarojini took him to the edge of the sea where the water died with a popping of rainbow bubbles, each wave bringing in a fresh supply.

Garry left them discovering the sea, and wandered down the beach. It was a working day and the stretch of sand was deserted. He wished he too was seeing the sea for the first time: their joy and wonder had wakened a wistful melancholy in him, like yearning to recall the smell of his first apple. Yet time past was a reminder of the transience of these dreamy days with Sarojini. He could not be like her and pick and choose only the melody she wanted to hear. For him, a false, discordant note crept into the music every now and again, and he lacked the innocence she had to be deaf to it. In the setting of the valley and the brilliant light of the sun, it was hard to shake off a feeling of unreality, that if they did not persist and persevere all would be lost. To make Sarojini aware of this would bewilder her: she took happiness as if it were her due, and there was enough for them both. Her shadow cast a shade for him to shelter from the burning sun, and she moved as he moved so that it always protected him, and he could bask in the cool while she made no demands on him. She was so happy that it frightened him; she was so bountiful in her love that it dwarfed his own feelings for her and made him wonder if he was capable of reciprocation. He was frightened, too, that any assessment or analysis might only sharpen him for disillusionment and grief. If they were under a magic spell . . . she had told him about Manko . . . why should he challenge it with doubt? In fact, as he thought of Manko, he remembered he wanted to go and see him, not to lift the veil, but to be reassured that the magic would not last for ever, for he did not have the capacity or the faith to stretch so far.

He turned to go back, taking up sea-coconuts . . . a round fruit like a golfball, and as hard . . . and tossing them to try and reach the breakers as they curled over in an arc of green and blue, pushing a fringe of seething white foam like a snowplough.

Sarojini hailed him, running down the beach with Dummy. She had taken off Kamalla's sari and folded it carefully and put it away; her slip was tucked into the elastic legs of her panties.

'Guess what, Garry,' she panted as they came up, 'I forget to bring a bathing suit.'

He laughed. 'You want my trunks?'

'What about up here?' She handled her breasts.

'The beach looks deserted. We could go in naked. Nobody would notice once you're in the water.'

'Teach me to swim Garry.'

'That'd take time.'

Dummy played a game with the sea coconuts strewn on the beach, rolling them as they went along.

'You could swim Garry?'

'A little.'

'I frighten if I drown!'

'I'll save you.'

'You won't. You would left me to drown and let the sharks eat me up. How big them waves is! What making them move? I taste the water, and it salty for so. I not coming back by the sea.'

'Oh?'

'Yes. It have so much space, that you go off by yourself and left poor-me-one.'

'I only walked down the beach. And you had Dummy.'

'Dummy ain't got what you got!' Mischievously, she made a grab at his genitals and as he started, she ran off screaming with laughter.

While they gambolled in the shallows Dummy made sand-things kneeling on the beach. It was almost as good as mud. With the coconuts and seaweeds and bits of flotsam, he built a house for Sarojini and Garry. Later, he spread out the lunch on dry coconut branches under the sea-almond tree, ready for them when they came out of the water.

While they were resting after eating, and Dummy was down the beach coaxing crabs out of their holes with a long stick, Garry said, 'When are we going to see Manko?'

'Tomorrow.'

'Seriously.' He knew what she meant. Some time in the distant future. 'There are some things I want to ask him.'

'For the book?'

'That, too.'

She was not anxious to visit the obeahman. He might take something away from her, shorten her happiness or divine trouble.

He said: 'I thought we could go this evening.'

'So soon!'

'What difference does it make.'

'I thought you was getting plenty notes from the people we went by.'

Her hesitancy mesmerized him again and he made a conscious effort to overcome it.

'A visit to Manko is overdue,' he said firmly. 'I thought he was your friend?'

'All right,' she said quickly, conscious of the slightest fractional change in his mood.

Small matter as the decision was, it was the first time they had talked about anything that caused the merest hint of uneasiness; aware of it, he said lightly, 'You afraid of the obeahman?'

'I not afraid of anything with you,' she said.

Dummy filled a coconut shell with some sea to take back to the village.

Manko lit the kerosene lamp and his shadow leapt like a giant geni from the ground to the *carat* roof of his hut. The geni materialized as head and feet only, no body, for there was only a four-foot wall, like a skirting, really, running around the circular hut, between the ground and the thatched roof. The wrong shape was most unusual, denoting African rather than East Indian origin: all the other huts for miles around, and perhaps the island were basically square or rectangular. Because of the low skirting it resembled a band-stand as those found in parks or city squares. Manko liked to be in the open and such a design satisfied him, being able to see all the surrounding forest, and great pieces of star-studded sky at night. He sometimes brought in a branch, or a complete tree, and propped them up in the corner: they helped to enhance his reputation as an obeahman at the same time. Also, because the mud floor was on a level with the earth, all manner of creatures came and went; once a *mapipire* snake spent a week in a corner, shedding skin before it left. There were no dividing walls, no doors, no windows, no screens. The state of the floor depended on weather conditions: Manko's bare feet brought in rusty, damp cacao leaves and mud. The roof had a large hole: it was no trouble to get a *carat* leaf, the bother was in climbing up there and fixing it. He had salvaged an iron bedstead from the servant's quarters at the big house, and this supported the planks of *crapaud* wood he slept on, with cocoa bags for bedding. There was a table and a chair, also from old furniture dumped from the house. He did his cooking, if any, in the yard, and out here he had a small shed where he kept his obeah paraphernalia to fool people. In the beginning he was quite honest about his powers and sprinkled a little elementary psychology with a dash of common sense. But 'rattle the bones, Manko,' and 'make your *seemeedeemee,* man. Burn bush. Call the spirits. Make sign in the dust. *Make obeah,* man!' He had a spare bag in the hut with some snake oil and jumbie beads and peacock feathers for common ailments and woes, and only went to the shed when he was hard-pushed by some stubborn customer he sincerely wanted to help. Not that there was anything in the shed to augment his powers, but resorting to it, he made it quite clear that if the treatment failed this time, monkey would smoke the sufferer's pipe, and not even *white* magic would help. This always effected a cure.

Apart from an occasional hunter passing that way in the night looking for *manicou* and *agouti,* perhaps a deer, the only casual visitor he ever had was Eloisa, who paid two visits at the same time, her first and her last. It was a long time ago, when she was younger and had a more active affection for him. Also, curiosity prompted her. All that talk about obeah and spirits. It happened that that was the morning the *mapipire* shed its skin, and when she saw it she fled without saying a word to Manko. Afterwards, in her terrified mind, the snake multiplied into all manner of creatures great and small, and she was convinced that Manko was Papa Bois, a legendary figure who befriended all the animals in the forest and led hunters astray.

But this evening, now, Manko knew he was going to have two visitors. He was amused by the stories that went about the estate and the village concerning the white man and Sarojini . . . even he could not concoct anything as fabulous and imaginative. Like how they wanted ritual and decoration with their cure, so they could not be satisfied with the simple knowledge that Sarojini and Garry were doing it together: they had to embellish and invent. This was partly to snicker at Prekash, who galloped about the estate like a madman, hoping to catch them at it. Manko offered to work a bit of obeah to sedate him, but the overseer blamed him for everything that was happening, and said that Manko wanted to poison him. A man so blatantly rejected, especially an ignorant one, was likely to be dangerous; Manko thought he should warn Sarojini when she came.

She brought him some of the food left over from Balandra Bay, and Garry had a bottle of Vat 19. Manko turned up the lamp and brought cups and opened the bottle. He poured a few drops in the corner . . . 'for luck,' he told Garry . . . before filling the cups. Outside, candle-flies made circles in the dark, their green, luminous eyes set like tiny emeralds, a yellow glow emanating from their bodies every now and then. Sarojini had brought one in with her. It was black, about an inch or so long and the wings were hard as scales.

Manko said, taking it from her, 'These candle-flies smarter than me. It will answer all your questions.' He held it up with two fingers, leaving the head free, to demonstrate. 'The first question you always ask is if someboly pee their bed. Mr Johnson does pee his bed?'

The head nodded with a click. Sarojini laughed and asked 'Manko does pee his bed?'

'Here you play with it. When the head don't move, the answer is no.'

Sarojini took it and went and sat on the bed, leaving the two men at the table. She did not want to talk with them. Manko might remember something bad to divine for her.

Manko caught Garry looking around and said, 'You rather stay in the big house, eh?'

'I expected an obeahman to look after himself.'

'What you don't have you don't miss. You get enough stories for your book?'

'People have been kind, going out of their way to help. What's the one about a *corbeau's* egg?'

'Ah, you hear that. They say if you get a *corbeau* egg . . . you know what a *corbeau* is? A vulture . . . good luck and wealth will be yours. It got people in Trinidad still searching for *corbeau* nest!'

'What sort of bird is it?'

'Funny you ain't seen one. They always about the place feeding on dead dog or cat. They only have to smell some-

think stinking and they come down from the sky in all
directions. In two-twos all that's left is bones.'

'You ever found a nest?'

Manko made a sound like a chuckle. 'You think if I had,
I would be here? First you got to boil an ordinary egg to
put in the place of the one you thief, else the corbeau will
chook out your eye.'

'I see. And what about the *douens*? Is it true they walk
backwards?'

Sarojini joined Garry on the floor, putting her arms around
him and resting her head on his shoulder. She put the candle-
fly down and it stayed still as if lifeless for a few moments,
then took off, belly glowing yellow, and flew outside.

'You want to hear a story about the *douens*?' Manko
filled his cup. 'When I was a little boy I was playing whoop
in the bush with my friends and I get lost. Lucky, I see foot-
prints in the mud, so I start to follow them, going back
because it had less bush that way. But it wasn't my friends
at all. It was a set of *douens*. They is children who never
been christened, and because of that, they have long hair
covering their faces, and their feet turn backwards, so when
you think from the footprint that they going one way, they
really going the opposite. Well, I was really frighten, but
they hold my hand and make me start to play with them.
They was really trying to lead me far into the forest, so lucky
thing my father come to look for me. When the *douens* see
him coming they run away. My father say that *douens* is
children who dead before they could christen. You know who
know about them?'

'Who?'

'Dummy. You ask him. He does play with them in the
bush.'

Garry handed Sarojini his empty cup and she filled it for
him.

They were quiet for a while. Garry had come with the
intention of learning about Manko's background. There was
no denying that he had remarkable powers, radiating an
almost hypnotic spell about him. Sarojini had been listening
entranced to every word.

Manko put the bottle in short pants with another drink

and said, I been trying to figure out what wrong with you, Mr Johnson. But I ain't get far.'

'Nothing wrong with Garry, Manko.'

'The signs say otherwise. Time speeding, speeding for him. Why?'

'We better go now,' Sarojini said, getting up.

'No.' Garry pulled her down. 'I want to find out.'

'I is the one who want to find out,' Manko said. 'Tell me.'

'Tell you what?'

'I know this much, that is something to do with your head.'

'I don't see nothing wrong with Garry head.' Sarojini examined it, parting the hair and looking closely. Garry pushed her hands away gently.

'God knows how you know,' he said slowly. 'I won't try to understand.'

'That's right. Just believe, or don't believe.'

'What wrong, Garry?' Sarojini was close to tears, overwhelmed by a feeling of dread. 'We shouldn't of come here tonight. Manko want to take back what he give us.'

'Nobody could do that,' Garry said softly, pacifying her, and he went on to explain about his wound simply and lightly, as if there was nothing to worry about, and did not mention how uncertain he could be for the future. But Manko knew, and confused herself, Sarojini looked to see the obeahman's reaction. Manko was going to say something when Garry stopped him with a sign.

'What it is?' Sarojini's fear sharpened her wits. 'The bullet still in your head, not so? The doctors them couldn't take it out?'

'It's nothing like a bullet.'

Manko shook his head slowly, and as slowly said, 'All those big brains in the world, London, America, Germany . . . none of them can't do nothing? They just left you to dead?'

'They tried everything. Maybe they'll come up with something one of these days.'

'Yes.' Manko looked at Sarojini. She was tugging at Garry, her face distorted with anguish.

'Garry, Garry! Something bad you and Manko hiding from me. You sick? What wrong?'

'Is nothing girl.' Manko spoke, as Garry remained silent.

'How is nothing? You think I fall off a tree? Garry have a bullet in his head waiting to kill him.' She burst into tears now, covering her face with her sari like Indian women in mourning.

'It's not as bad as it sounds.' Garry was upset to see her so distraught. 'Tell her Manko.'

'Sure, sure. Stop that bawling, girl. Ain't you seen some big six-inch rusty nail run up in a man foot, and we get it out? Just the other day a fellar came and say a rusty chip remain inside his leg, just below the knee, from an accident he had. And all I had to do was apply some aloes. That draw it out.'

'Aloes would draw out the bullet from Garry?' She asked jerkily, and then, her voice growing with desperate hope, she answered her own question. 'Yes, yes! Aloes would do it!'

'Well now, I ain't say so.' Manko gave Garry a glare to indicate it was all his fault.

Noticing it, Garry said, 'Listen, Sarojini . . .'

But before he could go any further she stopped him, her eyes wild and bright. 'If anything happen to you I will kill myself! Manko could save you, Garry. All that magic, all that obeah. It ain't got nothing Manko can't do. Aloes will do it, aloes will do it.'

Garry embraced her and she started to cry again, softer, in his shoulder. Garry looked helplessly at Manko.

'Tell her something. Anything.'

'I will have to do some consultations and some cogitations tonight, and let you know tomorrow. Come back in the morning.'

'Yes Manko.' Sarojini rubbed red eyes, trying to still her jerking body.

Manko took something from the pocket of a khaki trousers on the bed and brought it to her.

'Here. A donkey-eye, for luck.'

It was a hard, brown seed, shaped like a miniature jewel-case, with a black band running around the side. 'Keep it safe,' he said. 'Wear it all the time, and it will protect you. And make sure you don't mix it up with any others, because you won't be able to tell the difference.'

She took the donkey-eye and tied it in her sari. 'What about one for Garry?'

'That will do for the both of you.'

'And you want we to come back in the morning, after you talk with the spirits-them?'

'Sarojini,' Garry began.

'Yes yes,' Manko said impatiently, pushing them out of the hut, hoping they would find something better to do and leave him in peace.

'I'm sorry we troubled you,' Garry said, lingering as Sarojini went out. 'She believes you can do anything.'

'The question is, *you* believe?' And Manko gave him a little shove before he could say anything more.

A jumbie bird on its way to the *pepal* tree rested in a balata shadowing the hut and went who, who, who. Manko cleared his throat and fired phlegm at the sound.

Later that night he thought he should do some penance and suffer for daring to think he could challenge the spirits that had graced him with a little supernatural power. He, of all people, should know better than to stand on the shore and try to push back the waves, like some old scamp he had heard about long ago. He was constantly advocating acceptance of what was decreed and had to happen, yet here he was, tempted to pit his puny knowledge against the might of powers which controlled a man's mission. Was he getting too big for his skin? Had conceit made him overconfident. History was full of pupils who tried to better their masters and ran bawling for murder when they put their hands in the fire. *A chinky little bit of thing stick up in a man head, and all the big professors and inventors in the world couldn't do nothing! They sending men to the moon, they inventing babies, they making bombs what could wipe up the whole world, and a chinky bit of thing stick in a man head and causing panic and pandemonium! Any kiss-me-arse bush doctor could do that! Even Manko!* What if the spirits themselves had put the idea in his head, and had sent this white man all the way from England so that he, Manko, could put a spoke in the wheel?

He sat up and looked over the low wall. He had a starlit view of the small plot where he grew a few vegetables. And

. . . yes, he could see the aloes tree clearly. It was a kind of small cactus, with oval-shaped, fleshy protuberances . . . neither leaf nor branch . . . which shrivelled and dried when it bloomed, which was only once in a lifetime. And . . . he rubbed his eyes . . . it was in flower now, at the peak of life after years of struggling against the elements, and would die in a week or two. Surely this was a sign?

What hurt Prekash most was that he had done nothing with Sarojini. It was the bitter lump that stuck in his throat like a rock and stifled him. Not a feel-up, not a handsy, not even a sly pin-t at her panties. All the chances he had missed, in the cocoasheds, behind the house, sometimes at the hut in the village when Ramdeen wasn't there. All gone, and nothing to show for it but a frustrated prick. He ground his teeth when he thought of it. If he had had a little piece, in the mud or against a mossy cacao tree or even standing up. But she had pissed on him from a height, and that was the rub. Blatantly, shamelessly, flauntingly she showed him that a donkey had more chances of shitting round than he had of getting near to her. Yet, as the old calypso used to say, *one day one day congo-tay*! meaning to say that every dog shall have his day, even the mobile hatracks that scavenged in the village backyards. *One day one day congo-tay*! Everybody knew, everybody smirked and whispered and tittered. In the shop, drinking more than he could take, he tried to straighten his back, he told them Garry was only eating an orange he had sucked dry, riding a horse he had turned out of the stable. *And never so much as had a glimpse of leg or knee.* One day, one day. In the night he started out of sleep sweating and exhausted as if he had taken part, to find the pillow kneaded and misshapen between his legs.

In those burning days he found a surprising ally in Eloisa, of all people. At first he was suspicious as she commiserated and consoled, knowing too well that Trinidadians are masters of irony, and watched sharply for hidden laughter and secret meaning. But he began to drop around by the kitchen backsteps now and then and she would give him a glass of cold lime punch or mauby and bend a sympathetic ear.

'You think this should happen to me, Eloisa? I wait and wait all these years, and I never touch she, I swear Eloisa, she still had she maiden up to the time he come.'

And Eloisa: 'Don't listen to all the malicious talk. You know she's a good girl, Prekash.'

'Good girl?' He could hardly swallow the cold drink. 'You call that good girl, what she doing?'

'You ever seen them with your own two eyes?'

'Everybody seen them. She got no shame left. What you think they doing in the bush, catching bird?'

'You only fulling up your mind with stupidness. People got enough worries without imagining. And too besides, you getting on as if Mr Johnson going to stay in Sans Souci for ever. He got to go back to England, you know. He working on that book thing. He got a typer machine, click-click it go, and make up the stories. How else he would get them stories if Sarojini don't take him around tell me?'

'Next think you will say Sarojini writing book too!'

While others spread scandal, Eloisa was alarmed for the safety of Sarojini and Garry. Prekash was still a little boy to her, and that made it worse, no one could tell what mischief he might get up to. The Indians had a casual way of swinging a cutlass to level things out, as if they were cutting cane. She didn't like to see Prekash prowling about the estate wearing his cutlass . . . which he had not done since his promotion to overseer. That was why she tried to coax and solace him, before something evil befell. His bragging manners and false, superior airs had made him lonely and friendless, and if everybody turned a blind eye to his rage he might explode like a sandbox seed in the hot sun.

Prekash secretly thought Eloisa was an old cunt, but there was nobody else to talk to. Plans for violence mostly came when he could stand the torture no more: he saw their heads rolling on the ground if he ever came across them. But perhaps there was another solution. There were more ways than one of catching a parakeet. If he tackled the situation from an unexpected angle, he might still laugh last.

It was with this in mind that he went to find Ramdeen one morning. He was nowhere on the estate . . . not unusual

. . . and he saddled a horse and rode to the village, hoping to find him at the shop.

There were two or three alcoholics opening their eyes over a drink. Often, they drank through the night, spent an hour in nightmare sleep wherever they happened to be, and were waiting at the doors of the shop in the morning. The walled-off section where they drank had some tables and they found everything as they had left them the night before . . . the glasses, a bottle in short pants, cigarette ash and butts. 'It wasn't a goat, it was a pig.' They resumed conversation and drinks as if they had been there all the time. One of them said, when Prekash asked for Ramdeen, 'The bitch went home for some money and didn't come back.'

Prekash bought a bottle and went to the hut. He found Ramdeen malingering on a bench under the mango tree, with a chronic cough that all the older Indians seemed to suffer from, which they called *harpee*.

'The *harpee* acting up.' Ramdeen forestalled Prekash's query, and coughed several times to confirm it.

'*Harpee* my arse,' Prekash said. 'I want to have a serious talk with you Ramdeen.'

'Yes?' Ramdeen scrabbled around, found an empty bottle and flung it away in the bush with disgust. Prekash produced his bottle, and Ramdeen's face brightened. He took it from the younger man and unscrewed the cap, seal and all. As Prekash spoke he christened the bottle.

'This time not going to be like all the other times you keep making excuse about me and Sarojini marrieding.'

'Yes. But I sorry to say, Prekash, that it have to be, because things even worse than they was before. No improvement. She doesn't even say good morning.'

'I decide to wait. I won't bother to harangue and harrass you about that any more.'

'Good.' And Ramdeen got off to his first proverb: 'All things come to him what waits.' He remembered he had *harpee* and coughed. Prekash took a swig. 'Yes, I not in any great hurry anymore. Is that other business I come to talk about.'

'What other business?'

'Don't pretend you don't know. Sarojini and the white

man.' Even he was using the title by which the affair was known in the entire neighbourhood. Like if referring to the title of a book, the villagers talked of Sarojini and the White Man, the phrase all that was necessary these days to encompass the whole business.

'Oh. *That.*'

'Yes. *That.*'

'Give a man enough rope and he *heng* himself.' Ramdeen had another drink to celebrate the quote: it looked like a good morning for them. He nursed the bottle from Prekash, thinking up some more to sprinkle into the conversation.

'Your daughter, Ramdeen. Your own daughter. You not ashamed? Behaving like a George Street whore.' George Street is one of the whore streets in Port of Spain. 'You sit down there drinking my rum, as if you don't care what happens. What sort of father you is at all? You don't realize this thing leading to BIG trouble?'

'The white mister only here on holiday.' Ramdeen didn't even know Garry's name.

'Holiday? You know is almost three months now and he still here? Listen man. All of we is Indian together, right?'

'Birds of a feather,' Ramdeen began promptly, but it didn't sound right.

'Listen man,' Prekash said patiently, 'the thing is, think of our religion and customs, if nothing else. You don't see how bad it reflect on the whole Indian generation for this girl to fling sheself like that at a *white* man?'

'She would married Indian in the long run, don't worry. You, I mean. Still, that bad, boy. Is not a good example to set.'

'Exactly. Think how all the black people in the village must be saying that those coolies only go by the temple to pretend. I tell you, Ramdeen, these days I shame to lift my head in the street when I think of a Indian girl disgracing we so.'

'What we going to do, Prekash? You know how strong-headed the girl is. She doesn't even do *puja* in the temple no more.'

'That's it. And listen.' Prekash drew a deep breath to deliver the greatest threat of all. 'Suppose this girl take it in she head to *married* this white man?'

97

'What!' Ramdeen almost fell off the bench. The bottle rocked and he grabbed it quickly. 'What!'

'Is not impossible, you know.'

'Married!' Ramdeen said. The quote came without thinking: 'East is East, and West is West, and Never the Twain Shall Meet!'

'The twain done meet already. The twain look like if it going to tie up in a big knot what nobody could untie.'

'You think so? You really think so?' The matter was getting grave: he even suspended a drink.

'If you sit on your arse and do nothing, you will find out.'

'H'mm.' Ramdeen grew pensive: he took a thoughtful drink.

'And don't believe that if it happen, you get rich suddenly because she married white, with big house and car. They wouldn't even blink on you. They will take off like a bullet and left Trinidad.'

Yes, Ramdeen thought, Sarojini would do that. Alarmed at the prospect of a stoppage of monthly cash from the post office, he asked, 'What to do, Prekash, what to do?'

'I got an idea.'

'Yes.'

'In all the confusion and bacchanal, everybody forget what a good friend Mr Franklin is to all of we.'

'Yes, Prekash. A friend indeed is a friend in need.'

'If Mr Franklin get to find out what happening, he won't stand for no stupidness. Thing is he so busy these days he ain't have time to notice what going on. Somebody should tell him.'

'Ah, that's it.' Ramdeen snapped his fingers as if he had thought of it himself. 'Who shall bell the cat?'

'You. You is Sarojini father. Go and see Mr Franklin and tell him. Talk your mind. The sooner the better.'

'Yes,' Ramdeen said, and murmured to himself, 'A stitch in time saves nine.'

'You have to find a chance,' Prekash said. 'He hardly in office these days, but you sure to see him some time. Tell him everything. But don't mention my name.'

'All right, Prekash. I will take your advice to heart.'

'Good. Now, why the arse you didn't come to work today?'
'I tell you, Prekash, the *harpee*. Give a man a chance to catch my breath. You know what the old calypso say, All work and no play makes Jack a dull boy.'
You lazy drunken bastard, Prekash thought as he rode away, I hope you convince Mr Franklin and don't talk a set of shit and proverbs.

Garry had a restless night after the visit to Manko. He dreamt a gang of *douens* was after him and getting closer and closer, and somewhere Sarojini was screaming, 'Run backwards, Garry, run backwards!' He got up and lit a cigarette, and killed a mosquito which had been persistently buzzing in his ear. It was unusual for him to have disturbing dreams. He had trained himself long ago to shut off his mind when he went to bed and forget a tomorrow he might never see. He felt now he was being forced into planning and decisions. Believe what? Any belief suggested hope. Sarojini could not know what centuries of accepted precepts and concepts, dogmas and proven convictions enveloped someone like him, controlling his mind as rigidly as if it were set in concrete. And even given slack, how could he bring himself to hope an old black man, untutored and uncivilized, could help when the best medical resources had failed? This valley, those immortelle, the hot sun, the smell of ripening cocoa, Sarojini's clean innocence, and the legends and fantasies, things that moved and whispered and plotted in the dark . . . all these related to a condition of dream which he had accepted. Now his acceptance was being challenged. Was there a way out without shattering Sarojini? Perhaps he could submit merely to make her happy, and retain his reservations. What did he have to lose? Even in medical science they were realizing that certain primitive remedies had value . . . some root in the depths of the Amazon, some herb from darkest Africa. He had been told not to give up hope, every day there was a new drug, a new method, some discovery in another part of the world.
Unresolved, he dozed fitfully, and got out of bed with the first light of dawn. He showered, and was down for breakfast

before Roger, still unsettled, more so now wondering what Roger would say if he knew. Guiltily, he took a large drink to dullen his thoughts, and was having another when Roger came down.

'You want to keep off that stuff so early,' he said carelessly.

During breakfast he asked Garry if he would like to come to town.

'It might bore you, though, standing in the hot-sun in Woodford Square. The demonstration I told you about is this morning.'

'I thought it wasn't definite.'

'Up to me, there won't be any. It's costing the estate a day's labour at a bad time. The rainy season is about due and we haven't bagged the cocoa. How's your work coming?'

'Keeping me busy.'

'It's good you thought of that. Once this cacao-land business is settled I'll have more time. You're not in a hurry to get back to the cold, are you?'

'I ought to be thinking of it.'

'You have a date in mind?'

'Not really.' It was another decision he had to make.

'I only ask because if you're going back by boat, it's as well to book up in advance. I could do that for you, and get a ticket. You can always change the date if you like.'

'Yes, I'd rather a sea voyage.'

Roger finished quickly and rose from the table. 'I'm taking some of the men with me. Sure you don't want to come?'

'There's some Indian ceremony in the village today I'd like to see.'

Left alone, Garry sipped his cocoa and lit a cigarette. The reminder that he had only come to Sans Souci for a holiday made him realize how much he had put off thinking about that time. Perhaps it was because he and Sarojini would have to make a beginning they pretended had already happened. Last night had given them a glimpse of the first shadow, the first tear. Only *douens* could start their beginning at the end, and work backwards from death to birth.

When he met Sarojini, the shadow grew darker when he saw how distressed she looked.

'How you feeling, Garry?' She asked as if he might have died in the night.

'I'm all right, I told you not to worry. But you look as if you had no sleep.'

'I was in the temple yard. I pray all night, and left some flowers for the spirits.'

'You'll make me regret you found out.'

'Don't vex, Garry. I was thinking how I got nothing to give you, and you give me so much. What matter if I miss a little sleep? Too besides, my prayers answer. Manko will work good obeah.'

'Really Sarojini. You think we should go on with this? Last night . . .'

She put her fingers on his lips. 'Don't talk, Garry. Up to now everything was all right, because we don't talk, we know what we have in our minds. Talk will only bring misery. Just hold my hand and follow me.'

Manko was bending over a small, smoky fire in the yard when they arrived. He glanced up, but went on throwing some leaves in the flames and inhaling the fumes.

'Wait until he finish,' Sarojini whispered, putting a restraining hand on Garry.

'Is all right,' Manko said, overhearing, 'don't give Mr Johnson any false idea. He must be feel I doing this to impress him.'

'Why then?' Garry asked, seeing no other reason for the fire.

'These smells good to clear the brains. You want to try?' Manko stood up.

'I bring him, Manko, I bring him,' Sarojini sang out, and tried to push Garry forward, but he felt a little foolish, and loosened her hand. The heavy drinks before breakfast on an empty stomach made him sick now.

'So I see.' Manko looked keenly at him. 'Well, I ready. The thing is, *you* ready? Because if you ain't, if you don't believe, is no use going on.'

'Garry believe, Manko,' Sarojini said anxiously. 'You think we would of come if he didn't?'

'He don't look too happy to me.'

Feeling like a pawn, Garry said, 'What exactly do you think you can do?'

'I don't usually explain nothing to nobody. But then, I never had a white customer before.'

'I haven't much faith, in spite of what I think you can accomplish.'

'We wasting time talking,' the old man said. 'Is one thing or the other. Yes or no?'

'Maybe if you give me an idea what you want to do?'

'That will take away the magic.'

'I'll risk that.'

'All right. Come and see the aloes.'

Manko led them to the tree. He cut a small piece and peeled off the thick green covering. The flesh was colourless, almost transparent, and oozed a sticky moisture. Garry slid his fingers on it and smelt them. There was no odour.

'You know everybody head got a mole?'

'What's that?'

'A soft spot. In a baby you could see the pulse beating.'

'Oh yes.'

'Well, I going to make a small cut in your mole and put the aloes. It will draw out whatever in your head.'

'How?'

'You got to ask the aloes tree that one.'

'That's all?'

'Yes.'

'No!' Sarojini cried. 'Take him in the shed, Manko, and work big magic. You promise, Manko, you promise' She turned to Garry, pointing to the shed. 'Is in there he have all the business to work obeah. Make him take you in there, Garry!'

He was almost ready to give in about the aloes, but hesitated to commit himself any further.

Sarojini said, with an inspired logic, 'I doing the believing for you, Garry, and I won't believe unless Manko do magic. Please Garry please. You don't understand these things. I know you think is stupidness, but do it for my sake.'

'All right.' He shrugged. 'I'm only fooling myself by accepting part of the whole. If it makes you happy I'll do it.'

Instantly the gloom and anxiety fled from her; it almost embarrassed him to see how joyous she became at such little sacrifice on his part.

'What I could do to help, Manko, anything?' She asked.
'Yes. You keep the fire going while we in the shed. Here.'
He gave her some dry leaves, and a small tin of black powder.
'Put these in the fire slow, bit by bit. And remember, if you
let the fire out, only one of we going to come back out of that
shed.' He beckoned to Garry and they went into the tiny
shack. There was hardly any room to move, and coming
in from the glare he could not see anything. Manko pulled
the door and shut out all light. Garry could hear him breathing in the dark.
'You frighten?'
'Only curious. What do you keep in here?'
'Hold this for me whilst I light the candle.' Manko shoved
something smooth and round in Garry's hand. When the
candle flared he saw it was a small human skull and started
involuntarily.
Manko laughed, a rare sound for him. 'You frighten, eh? I
was always longing to get a white man in my power, to get
some samples of blood. I hear it's blue.'
'Mine is red, same as yours.'
'If you was dying and I was the onlyest man with blood
to give you a transfusion?'
'I don't think we have enough light in here,' Garry said.
There was a change in Manko's tone and demeanour, perhaps to be expected.
'It will do. I will fix you up good so nobody would know
or see anything suspicious. While I working you can look
around you and amuse your eyes.'
He sat Garry on a box. He tipped the candle so that some
drops of oil fell on the skull and he stuck the candle there
to stand before the oil could harden.
'Just hold the light while I tend to you. A small cut what
you won't even feel.'
Garry held the skull gingerly. Manko searched his head
and found the spot and made the incision without further
preliminary. It did not hurt; Garry could hardly feel his
touch as he worked.
'That skeleton you holding belong to a *douen*.'
'If you leave the door open you'll have better light to see
what you're doing.'

103

'Who working this obeah, you or me?'

It seemed they were talking to each other, but could not make a connection. Garry already regretted coming. He should have gone to town with Roger, taken a day off from the constancy of Sarojini, the vivid compulsion of the valley.

'You think this aloes will really work, Manko?'

'That's up to you. You should let me learn you how to work obeah. You could go back to England and fool up them white people.'

'They don't fool so easy.'

'I fool you.'

'No.'

'No? Then you fool yourself.'

'You're a different man when you're surrounded by your magic herbs and concoctions.'

'Wait till we come to the obeah part. I got to rattle my bones and chant some spells and give you some potions to drink. Else you would feel I cheating.'

Garry said, 'Why are you telling me all this?'

'Because I know you don't believe none of it. I could fool you, but *you* can't fool *me*. Still, the experience would make a good story for your book. Imagine how you must be pay all them scientists and professors a thousand dollars, and you got to pay me nothing. I finish now.'

'Is that all?'

'Yes. We will leave the obeah for another day. You got to come back to change the dressing and put a fresh piece of aloes.'

'Wait now, you didn't tell me that.'

'Sarojini could do it for you if you don't want to come back.' It seemed as if, for no apparent reason, Manko had lost interest in what he was doing. He blew out the candle and kicked open the door.

The sudden glare made Garry blink and rub his eyes. He was streaming with sweat, and the breeze that came in was cold on his wet skin. Depression overwhelmed him, a strange emptiness engendered by the thought that he had let himself down by going through with the ridiculous farce, even shorn of beads and bone-rattling. All that Manko had done was to demonstrate a cold, disinterested superiority. What would he have done with someone who believed? He wondered what Roger would say if he knew; he was irked by a feeling that in some inexplicable way he had let Roger down by indulging in this confidence with the natives . . . and with the thought, he realized he had used the word 'natives' for the first time.

Manko felt he had made a grave mistake trying to treat this white man. He slunk into the hut, leaving him alone with Sarojini in the yard: it was all her fault that he was in trouble now with the spirits.

But the girl kneeling by the fire believed. She had not budged from that position, and had stoked the fire far more than necessary to keep the flames burning.

5

Later that morning the drummers had a small fire going, doing their own kind of magic . . . tuning their instruments. The heat stretched the goatskin of the drums, and they slackened or tightened it as they tested, beating the surface with the flat palms of their hands or with short sticks bound with cloth at the end. The tuning was important. The sounds they strived for depended on the ceremony, each one requiring certain subtleties of rhythm and volume which would be peculiar to itself. The villagers were able to say what was happening merely by listening.

They were gathered in the yard in front of the shop, and the tuning was accompanied by much drinking for the drummers themselves to warm up. At such times they came into their own, for drumming was the heart of the ceremony, and the cluster of villagers kept them supplied with a steady flow. No drummer gave of his best until he was charged up with liquor, and once primed, could go on beating tirelessly for hours in the hot sun. Already their eyes were red and they were working themselves up to the high degree of concentration necessary to maintain and introduce certain changes of rhythm which required precision and exact timing. The untrained ear might hear only a monotonous, deafening, hypnotizing thump and thud, but let one drummer falter or mistime and the whole band would be thrown out of tune. You either had drumming in your blood or you didn't: there was no learning the art even by constant practice: some indefinable quality had to move in you so that you became an extension of the instrument and totally immersed. Now, there were a few boys hovering about, stoking the fire or running into the shop to bring drinks, or reverently examining the drums. These might be the drummers of tomorrow. By watching and listening they learnt a little, and by and by, they would be given a chance to play, or even to hold the drum while a player had a drink.

Sarojini stood with Kamalla among a group of women. She had left Garry to go and borrow a pair of panties from Kamalla . . . the last time, she promised her friend . . . and he was to join her later in the village to witness the ceremony.

Apart from the drummers and a few men who lingered about, the crowd was mostly women in gay saris. It was obvious, from the lack of solemnity, that this was going to be some sort of celebration rather than religious ceremony. One of them was going to be married in a few days, and it was a sort of female stag party. Accompanied by the drummers, the women were going to walk through the village and go to some secret spot in the bush where they would perform a ritual fertility dance asking the gods to bless the betrothed with children and prosperity. Like a great many customs, this one had borrowed bits and pieces from others until it was nothing like the original version. Many people did not know or care about the reasons or authenticity of rites, and certain aspects were modified or magnified. One of these now was that men were forbidden to witness the dancing, drummers excepted. By such intrigue, and employing any means to mystify or make more esoteric these observations, the pundit sought to keep the villagers' interest from waning. If too long a period came between two ceremonies, he invented one. He rode about on his bicycle at least once a day, the big black umbrella spread like an immortelle over his head for all to see him. Like all the Indians of the island, those in Sans Souci were lured by Western influences, and he injected mystery and spiced rituals with a little excitement lest he became expendable. The women were his main support. At the least sign of drought, or a poor crop or illness, he got them bustling about with prayers and collections of rice and flour to appease the spirits. This morning he left them alone, knowing his presence would lend an unwelcome austerity to proceedings.

Ramdeen, the acknowledged head drummer, arrived and surveyed his band. He shook his head dubiously, or nodded encouragement as they looked at him for a glance of praise or pleasure. His fame with the drums was island-wide. Sometimes there were competitions among the villagers, and the band travelled about, leaving the drums of Sans Souci resounding in the ears of their rivals.

Ramdeen took his drum and slung the leather strap around his shoulder: when the pace grew hot, he would place a piece of cloth between the strap and his body to ease the weight. A silence fell as the others deferred to the master. Ramdeen slapped the big drum. After that his hands moved so quickly they were only blurs from the wrist downwards. He shut his eyes and signalled the others to join him. Somebody thrust a glass of rum in front of him but he shook his head angrily; it was time they knew that the one thing he did not mix was drumming and drinking, especially as he was always charged up before he took over.

'Say what you like about your father, girl,' Kamalla said, 'but he could really beat drum.'

'That's the only thing he could do,' Sarojini replied. She wished he had gone to Port of Spain for the demonstration, like the other workers. Not that it made the least difference to her, but in a state of drunkenness heightened by the drums, he might cause trouble. She shrugged that from her mind and wondered what was keeping Garry. At the thought she realized she did not know the exact spot where the dance was to be held, and asked Kamalla.

'You know that clump of bamboo near the river, the first one you come to?'

'By the big rose-mango tree?'

'Yes.'

Sarojini said, with a pause, 'Kamalla. You think is all right if Garry come?'

'It sure to have some peepers,' Kamalla giggled at the idea, 'but that man is a stranger, you know?'

'Because he white?'

'Yes. I myself don't like the idea,' she lied. 'I mean, you got to draw the line somewhere, Sarojini. Is all well and good to have a little wetness in the bush, but things like we customs and habits you should leave him out of.'

'Why?' Sarojini demanded hotly. 'He *want* to know about them. He not just interested in wetness, as you say.'

'Garry's interest in the village pleased her. There was something personal and endearing . . . and hopeful? . . . in their relationship now. He asked questions about Ramdeen, he asked if she had other relatives, he asked what she did when she was not with him or on the estate. She was ashamed of her poverty and kept him away from her hut. Once he had asked her why she didn't wear shoes (sometimes Kamalla did to show off) and she laughed the question away. He did not know that every night she washed the little clothing she possessed, or borrowed from Kamalla.

She flushed at the crude suggestion, and Kamalla went on, 'What you trying to say, he going to married you? He going to start wearing dhoti and talk Hindi? Is time you come to your senses, girl. Don't put your hat so high you can't reach it.'

'You don't know nothing Kamalla. You never been in love. You only talking so because you been drinking.'

'You want some?' Kamalla taunted her with the bottle she had been sharing with some of the other women.

But Sarojini moved away, and looked up the street to see if Garry was coming. She wiped tears from her eyes. How cruel people were. Jealous and envious the moment good fortune came to her. Even the gods, making Garry think something was wrong with his head. But that was all right now, Manko's magic would work. She clutched the donkey-eye in her sari . . . and there was Garry in the distance, and Dummy running to meet him.

The crowd moved off, and some of the bolder women, including Kamalla, started to prance about in front, impatient to get going. In this vanguard were most of the older ones, shaking their flabby breasts and coaxing their heavy bottoms to wriggle as they demonstrated to the bashful, younger girls. They threw flowers, or broke a branch of leaf or blossom on the way. To perform at this function was good luck for un-married women: the one who outdanced the others was assured of a husband.

Sarojini waited behind for Garry, her hand clammy on the donkey-eye. She saw him searching in the crowd as he stepped to the side of the road. He had to jump over the drain into a patch of pumpkin vine as they came. With shrieks of laughter, led by Kamalla, the girls followed and smothered him with their saris, pulling at his arms and hair. Kamalla stood directly in front of him and jerked her waist suggestively.

It was very different from the morning the white man danced the cocoa with them and they blushed and hung their heads. Sarojini had shown them that even though he was white he was just like any other man, and wanted it just as badly.

'Garry!'

'Garry-oh, come and dance with we!'

'Garry do-do, what Sarojini got that I ain't got?'

He realized it was playful fun but tried to get away, his efforts hampered by the drain. By the time Sarojini came running up they had moved on, to catch up with the drummers.

She was furious. 'Garry! What happen?'

He crossed the drain and brushed his trousers. 'Nothing. Just a bit of skylarking.'

'They had no right!' She was very angry. Garry belonged to her, not to every woman in the village. She was sure Kamalla had put them up to it. 'They getting too familiar with themselves!'

'It was nothing.'

She calmed down. 'I don't know how you going to see the dance. Is for women only.' She squeezed the donkey-eye hard. 'Unless you hide somewhere.'

'There's a lot of bush.'

'No. Wait, you could climb up the rose-mango tree! Dummy will show you! You got to be quiet, though. Come.'

As they went along she pointed to the tree in the distance and to Garry, making signs to explain to Dummy what she wanted him to do.

She left them when they came to a bend in the track, and ran to meet the others. Dummy held Garry's hand and led him off the track, through clumps of guava and wild sage. The drums sounded loud when they got to the tree.

Dummy went up like a monkey and left Garry to his own resources. It was not difficult to climb. The trunk was rough and knotty and the branches not far apart: in a minute he was at the top, panting a little. They were surrounded by leaves and ripe mangoes which they had to push aside to get any view.

Though he could hear the drums getting nearer, Garry could not see anything. The spot was about halfway between the village and the estate, and instead of one grove of bamboo it seemed a long irregular line of it following the course of the riverbank.

The drums ceased abruptly, and Dummy nudged him and pointed. He saw the women as they broke through the bush and came into a small clearing strewn with dry bamboo leaves. They stood about chattering and laughing. The drummers chose the best shade, and one of them lit a fire for the drums. A bottle of rum went around and they caught mouthfuls without it touching their lips. Garry saw Sarojini look in their direction; he wished there was some way he could indicate they were safely in the tree.

For a while nothing happened, then the drums started and the older women came forward and began to dance, displaying all the traditional movements to the younger ones. Then the drums took a higher note and the girls joined in. Soon the elders left them to it and went and sat and clapped their hands in time. In between the whirling and spinning Garry caught the flash of Sarojini's sari. For a while there were too many for him to distinguish the movements, though they were wilder and more abandoned now in mood. As the dance was stripped of any pretence of modesty, they jerked and twisted in gyrations of the sex act, until one by one they began to retire, laughing and making remarks Garry could not hear, leaving only Kamalla and Sarojini to vie with each other. Kamalla was obviously the favourite because of her daring display, and as they shouted encouragement she went on to crudities which she knew Sarojini would be too modest to follow.

But Sarojini was dancing for Garry alone. Sometimes she was in the light and sometimes in the shadow, but she danced with her back to the others most of the time, and flung her head back to look up into the rose-mango tree. She moved further and further away, and suddenly she darted into the bushes and disappeared. There were cries of derision and mocking laughing. They gathered about Kamalla, as if proclaiming her the winner.

Sarojini raced through the bush, her sari flying behind her. By the time she got to the tree Garry and Dummy had come down, but Dummy returned to his perch when she appeared.

'What happened?' Garry asked her. Entranced by the ritual, he was yet puzzled by the obvious enmity towards Sarojini, as if all the other women had ganged up against her.

She was breathless. 'Come,' she said, taking his hand.

They walked for a while making their own way until they came to a clump of blacksage. He could sense some urgency and excitement in her, but even so he was not prepared when halfway through the blacksage she flung herself on him and bore him to the ground. She was wet with sweat, she smelt like an animal in heat. He himself was dripping, and there was no shade here from the pouring sun overhead . . . what shelter the sage offered was only from the eyes of passers by who might be straying that way.

She fought like a tiger in a net, with an amazing strength he never thought she possessed. Exerting only enough effort to barely keep her at bay, it suddenly struck him that her fury and passion were past the limits of frenzied desire and he was being called upon to use extraordinary force to control her. He clamped his mouth on hers and she took his tongue like a suction and bit it so hard he had to grab the roots of her hair and try to jerk her head away without hurting himself. It was too painful to experience any pleasure. He turned away and spat blood but she did not give him a chance. She sank her teeth in his throat and he had to almost throttle her before she would let go. She clawed at his shirt and her nails left red weals on his chest. Incongruously, it flashed on his mind how she had been like a child with her first set of crayons when she discovered that she could write or draw with her fingernails on his pale white skin, and the letters or picture would appear as the blood circulated into the marks she made. But this, now, was like fighting for his life. There was no room for one drop of desire in his thoughts: the moment his hands sought a caress she sensed his relaxation and started anew with feet and nails and teeth like the spring of a clock gone mad with overwinding. Her sari was loose and open and her breasts rose and fell as if the hardened teats were stabbing at him. He pinned her down, but was afraid to kiss her. Instead his lips sought her nipples and he bit them hard to make her moan and twist. Still he could feel her coiled and tense beneath him. She grew limp: he eased his hold, and with a supreme effort she rolled from under him and leapt on top. He lay there as if in surrender, but cautious. Her mouth opened to kiss him but he twisted his neck quickly and her lips fell on his cheek. They slid along his face, questing for his mouth, found it and locked. They began then, or Sarojini began, as if she had brought the true dance with her, loving him with tenderness and a certain dignity, quietening yet rousing his desire, stirring him with promise of pleasure when she felt he was ready. Her fingers danced on his body, her lips following wherever they went, until there was a glow in him from head to foot and he felt he would come on himself if he did not get her under him and begin to return her gifts. But she would take nothing from him: she pressed him down yet, and it was as if they were going to die together in a quiescent, hallowed climax such as he had never experienced before, and his whole being cried out in protest at the squander of such unparalleled delight. Then she laughed and the music changed and he was in a wonderment that she still had fight in her. But the fight now was gentle as she pleasured him with a variety of movement and touch as they worked to a simultaneous burst of splendour.

They were so exhausted they fell into a kind of swoon afterwards. After a few minutes Garry opened his eyes into the sun directly overhead. His body was on fire, baked brown all over except for the unconscious protection of Sarojini's arm across his chest, and here, their sweats mingled and collected like a dam.

As he shifted gently he broke the dam and a long pool of sweat literally ran like water.

When Sarojini fled from the dance Kamalla was bitterly disappointed. It robbed her of the moment of triumph she had anticipated, standing over a subdued and humble Sarojini. She had made up her mind to prove that all Sarojini had was looks. Now, though the other women accepted her victory, she was not satisfied. Indeed, by running away and not staying to take her blows like a man, Sarojini had made the whole affair a mockery and a sham, leaving Kamalla with the hollow feeling that the tables had been turned and that Sarojini had emerged with more grace from the marathon. The bitch. The thought rankled as they came from the bamboo and headed for the temple to conclude the ceremony. Before Garry came to Sans Souci it was Kamalla who held the stage in the village, and she did not mind sharing it in the beginning with her friend. But it was becoming monotonous to hear the name on every lip. Like a recurring decimal. She brooded all the way to the temple, taking no part in the chatter, or bothering to keep in step with the drummers. There was a sour taste in her mouth and she spat. The bitch had made her look like a fool, refusing to let herself go, as if to show she was too decent for that sort of wanton display Kamalla was giving. And all the time the brazen bitch was going about openly with the white man, pretending that nothing was going on, as if people were so stupid. And so blooming poor she had to borrow clothes to wear.

Kamalla was seething when they got to the temple. A few villagers had gathered to watch them, and the drummers dispersed among them, their duty finished.

Kamalla saw the bitch and the white man standing apart, waiting, as if they were too good to mingle with the common villagers. Standing up there like a saint, as if butter wouldn't melt in her mouth.

She strode up to them and said loudly, 'You run from the dance, girl! What happen, you couldn't stand the pace?'

Sarojini pretended not to hear, but the women followed Kamalla and she and Garry found themselves surrounded. Like *corbeaux* scenting carrion a crowd gathered in excited anticipation, wedging the couple so they couldn't move. Garry did not like the mood nor the glances of amusement they gave him as he stood uneasily in their midst. He thought at first it was all in good humour, but there was an edge of sarcasm as remarks began to come in from all sides.

'What happen to you, Sarojini, cat cut your tongue?'

'You frighten for your white man or what?'

'If Sarojini was my woman, I wouldn't let Kamalla talk to she so!'

Emboldened by the presence of each other, they seized the opportunity to harass the white man to see how he would react to the situation.

Sarojini tried to move away but they pressed even closer. 'Why you-all don't go about your business?' she said angrily. 'You want me to report the whole set of you to Mr Franklin?'

It would have been better to remain silent, this only brought derisive laughter and hoots. Garry had never seen them in a mood like this. Once, strolling through the village on his own, he had witnessed a quarrel and a fight between husband and wife in the road, but that had been an uninhibited, violent scene which somehow cleared the air, and afterwards husband and wife were having a drink together in the shop giving individual versions of the issue. But the people now were deliberately baiting Sarojini and himself. Was it because they suspected he had seen the ritual and resented it? Was it delayed reaction against his relationship with Sarojini?

'Let's get away from here,' he told her, holding her arm. But again no one would move to let them pass. Sarojini looked for a friendly face and saw none.

'What happening to you people here today?' It was the first time in her life that she was ever in a situation like this and it frightened her. The donkey-eye, knotted in an end of her sari, was moist in her clenched fist. 'You all gone mad or what?'

For a moment it appeared as if they would drift away, that Kamalla had only made a grandcharge and was depending on support from them that would lead to some form of action. But one hopeful egged her on now: 'What she do to you, Kamalla? Tell me what she do!'

'She too cheap to buy she own clothes, that's what!' Kamalla was obsessed with humiliating Sarojini. 'Every day she coming by me to borrow this, and borrow that, as if the white man don't give she nothing!'

115

It was hard to tell which of the two, Sarojini or Garry, was more embarrassed. Sarojini might have rallied if Garry was not present: it was his being there that brought a crimson flush to her face, she felt pulses throbbing all over her body.

Garry was struck dumb for a moment, and when he found voice and said, 'Come now, Kamalla, calm yourself,' the words sounded stupid.

Kamalla ignored him completely. Arms akimbo, she glared at Sarojini's bowed head and hand-covered face as she tried to hide her shame.

'Furthermore,' she screamed, 'she got on something now that belong to me!'

'Ah!'

'Oh!'

'What it is, the sari?'

The exclamations came fast, like rapid pistol shots of speculation contributing to Sarojini's humility and downfall.

'Here you are.' Garry took out some money and proffered it, 'How much is it?'

But Kamalla pushed his hand roughly aside, and again, his words sounded out of place, incongruous, as if he spoke another language, as if he could make no dialogue that would have sequence or meaning to these people.

'Furthermore Miss Sarojini, I want it back now, right here and now, this very minute, you hear?' She had advanced on Sarojini and was so close her voice roared in the girl's ear: Sarojini wished the roaring could be magnified and overwhelm her.

And then, with every eye in the crowd upon her, she bent and slipped her hands up from the bottom of her sari. She looked steadfastly at Kamalla as she shrugged her waist and pulled down the panties, doing everything quickly and with dignity, even to the awkward part of getting it from around her ankles. By the time the scandalized on-lookers realized what she was doing it was off and she flung it in Kamalla's face. They moved aside now and she walked off, and Garry followed her.

He heard the hubbub behind them, feeling inadequate and stupefied, not knowing what to do, or say, holding Sarojini's hand and it was lifeless and limp and cold, her head turned from him and downwards so he could not see her shame. Kamalla held the red panties over her head in both hands, displaying a ragged rent in one leg.

'That tear didn't happen when she was taking it off,' she said meaningfully. 'Who could guess where she went, and what she was doing, when she run away from the dance?'

Roger came back from the demonstration swearing it was going to be the last time he allowed himself to be drawn into anything to discuss anything with anybody anywhere. That was how Devertie had put it, in the ponderous, expansive way Trinidadians have of embracing the world and its population when they make their declarations: a basin of water was enough for Pontius Pilate, but he had to wash his hands in the Atlantic.

However it was put, the situation had reached a stalemate. Even as the demonstrators were marching in the streets a Government committee was being set up to study the problem. They, in turn, would wait the findings of a sub-committee. The matter might drag on into months, and already so much time had been wasted in discussions of a foregone conclusion.

The demonstration did not seem to have served any useful purpose. The cocoa proprietors had been informed of the government's intention at a meeting in Trinidad House that very morning. They had stayed on in the office to decide on one delegate who would represent their interests at further government meetings. Roger firmly declined, and now Devertie was making his stand. Roger knew what would happen. In the end, after a great deal of talk, Devertie would have to back down and take the nomination. The old cocoa-man was no fool. He knew that it had to be either Roger or himself, for their interests to be safeguarded.

Roger left them while they were still some way from this decision. He lunched at a Chinese restaurant in Frederick street, where Prekash came to pick him up in the Land-Rover. The rest of the men were left to find their own way by taxi or slow bus back to Sans Souci. It was not often, even in normal circumstances, that they visited the city, and in their own small way they would paint the town red and go back to the village with stories almost as incredible as Manko's tales.

'It had a man from the *Guardian* what take a lot of photos,' Prekash said when they were on the way. 'It should be in the papers tomorrow.'

'A lot of good that'll do,' Roger grunted. He had lunched lavishly, accustomed to Eloisa's heavy hand, and enjoyed a meal out now and then for a change: she would sniff contemptuously if she knew. He slouched back, relieved to have Prekash do the driving. He was very tired. He dozed through Success Village and Barataria, his mind eased of the land dispute, but other things coming into focus now as he had a chance to catch up with personal matters.

He woke to wipe the sweat lubricating the back of his neck against the seat.

'How many bags we've got, Prekash?'

'Nearly a thousand. I didn't finish checking.'

'H'mm.' It was going to be a good crop. 'You haven't got any more pods drying? The rainy season is here, you know.'

'All finished,' Prekash said with a note of pride in his competence.

'Start getting them out.'

'I start already, Mr Franklin. Twelve truckloads gone. We might of finish off today if wasn't for this demonstration.'

'Good.' Roger thought of trying to snooze again, but it was too hot, even though they were under way. Prekash was a nervous driver and he wished Roger would stop talking and give him a chance to concentrate. At one stage of his life he had considered, like so many Indians, driving a taxi for a livelihood, but he did not have the courage or stamina to flirt with death on the Trinidad roads.

'I haven't been spending much time with Garry. Has he been all right?'

'Oh yes.' Prekash answered without thinking. But he realized this was a chance he might be able to drop a hint or two to Roger, if he was careful. 'That's to say, I been so busy with the crop myself. But Sarojini been going around with him.'

'Sarojini?'

'Yes.'

Roger took his pipe from the dashboard and filled it slowly. How beautiful Sarojini had looked that morning in the blue and gold sari, stirring up the dust of the past. He had not seen her in it that first time when she danced the cocoa with Garry. He thought she was going to the ceremony that Garry had told him about at breakfast, and that was why she had dressed up. Imagine, she was old and big enough to wear her mother's sari. How quickly the years had gone by: they should have burnt her body on the banks of the Caroni in that sari: it had transfixed him this morning, in the yard, to see the daughter wearing it, he had thought it was the mother for a moment, come back to say he should not worry any more: that: that he: that he was: he had turned his back on it, and walked towards the Land-Rover where his men were waiting for him.

He thought, now, dreaming is a solitary thing, Garry dreams, I dream, and when two dreamers meet, one must come to earth. He saw it all in a flash: it irked him that he had to confirm his knowledge by asking Prekash, reviving the past with a careful nonchalance, lighting the pipe as a physical aid, 'Wasn't there some talk at some time about you marrying Sarojini?'

'You know how they like to spread gossip in Sans Souci. They even saying things about she and Garry.'

'What things?' He used sharpness in tone.

'Oh, I doesn't listen to them.'

'Don't lie to me, boy.'

The harsh, abrupt reprimand, so unlike Mr Franklin, almost made Prekash bump into a taxi which had stopped without warning. If Roger wasn't with him Prekash would have cursed the driver's mother's arse or cunt.

'All right.' Very quietly now. 'Keep your eyes on the road and concentrate on the driving.'

Prekash knew he had put a spoke in the wheel. The knowledge made him drive, not more carefully, but with wider eyes for the frantic traffic.

It is not really true that in a small community everybody knows your business. Privacy may be more difficult, and scandal-mongers may work overtime, but it is not altogether impossible to keep a secret. What is true is that everybody *thinks* they know your business, which is a different thing altogether. Like everybody *thought* Ramdeen was catching his arse, but there he was drawing an allowance every month; and everbody *thought* Manko was an obeahman, but he knew different; and everybody *thought* Prekash would ambush Garry and Sarojini in the cacao and chop off their heads with a cutlass, when he had subtler plans.

Everybody *thought* Kamalla was the village whore, and she did nothing to erase the impression. In fact, she knew that the best way to keep a secret was to pretend to have one, or give the village something to talk about. It did not matter what it was, and nobody was going to investigate the validity of any rumour or gossip: that it existed was sufficient, and the more scandalous and colourful the story, the happier the villagers. No one escaped, one felt left out if nobody had anything to say about one's way of life. It was also the practice to pin down one unfortunate victim whenever possible so that the others could indulge their privacy in a little peace. The current topic, Sarojini and the White Man, was exceptionally dramatic and intriguing and looked like settling down for a long run.

It gave Kamalla time to muse a little wistfully that she herself could have created even greater scandal if she wanted. The rub was not jealousy for Sarojini's luck, but envy that she had the spirit and the courage to flaunt it. All the glory and excitement heaped on Sarojini could have been hers long ago. People would have held their heads and bawled, her story would have stayed alive for years, a folktale related by old men over ganja pipes when work was over: told to children when candleflies flickered in the gloaming and smoky fires were lit to keep away mosquitoes; when men's memories were lubricated with rum and they were finished with the trivial anecdotes of their own prosaic lives. Her name might even have been a byword by now: 'But look at Sarojini! She playing she is *Kamalla* or what?'

As it was, she had kept her secret too well. It was possible that when the mark bust . . . truth came out . . . not a soul would believe this business had been happening under their noses and nobody suspected!

That was some consolation, she thought doubtfully as she prepared herself for the evening. She lived alone, in a small hut set apart from the others. Behind the hut was a large barrel of water in which a calabash shell floated, with a used cake of Lux soap in it. She kept the soap in the shell to remind her to use it when washing. She took off her clothes in the twilight and put them on the window ledge above the barrel. She washed carefully, scooping water with the calabash, and soaping herself twice under the arms and between her legs. There were marks all over her body where he had bitten her, like a hungry dog gnawing a bone. But it was a beautiful body. God had only forgotten her face.

She dried herself in the hut, using a fresh towel. She would have liked to use talcum powder, and spray herself with eau de cologne, but he had forbidden the use of any accessories. He wanted nothing but body smell. She put on new panties and bras from a chest of-drawers in the corner. It was filled with clothing: each time he came she had to put on fresh clothes, and he wanted her to throw them away afterwards, but she kept them for work, or to give Sarojini. She put on a clean dress and combed her hair, turning up the lamp for more light. Then she tidied the hut, and spread a clean blanket on the floor.

She blew out the lamp and lay on the blanket to wait. He wanted total darkness. Once she protested that as she wasn't sure exactly what hour he would be coming, she could not remain alone in the dark. But he did not mind if she slept: in fact, she had a feeling he preferred it that way, slinking in like an animal in the dark: sometimes she pretended sleep to give him greater kicks.

She must have fallen asleep now, for she did not hear him come. Suddenly he was on top of her, clawing like a beast, hot and panting for another rape. She lay quite still, with no response. He ripped her clothes off and drove into her with shocking force before she was ready. But that was the way it always was, she was conditioned to his craze, and even aroused she was fearful to make the slightest movement until he was exhausted and collapsed, and then she wriggled to ease her cramps and waited to see if he wanted more. After, without a word, he would slink away into the bushes as he had come.

Now, as she waited for another mount, she was startled to hear him speak.

'What is happening with Sarojini.' The voice had so much authority that questioning was unnecessary.

'What . . .'

'Think before answering.' He aborted the useless stalling he knew she would indulge in before he got a reply.

After a pause she said, 'She going with Mr Johnson. That's what you mean?'

'You sure.'

'Yes.'

'How long.'

'Since the day he come to Sans Souci they been doing it.'

'Stop it.'

'Stop it!'

'Yes. You could give him what he wants.'

She paused, then said, awkwardly, 'They in love.'

'You don't know what you're talking about.'

'Is true. Romance, like in the pictures.'

Well, he thought, it was a complication, perhaps more than that, a disaster. It was some satisfaction to know she wasn't whoring after Garry. How could such a thing happen in Sans Souci without him knowing? *Because he didn't want to know.* People woke from dreams and spent today thinking about yesterday and tomorrow: whichever way you looked at some threadbare scrap of philosophy, however you tried to refashion a tenet or a theory, time still moved and lives evolved. Sarojini could not stay stunted in the past awaiting his convenience to blossom forth. He was glad, in a way, that events had brought a reckoning to hand.

Kamalla was puzzled. Like an animal trained to the crack of a whip, she was bewildered by this diversion from the routine. Deep down in her, years of colonial servitude had roots that nothing simple like the island's independence or the cry of black power could eradicate. If, instead of an occasional fuck, he had desired the moon, she would have said yes sir and worry about it afterwards. Perhaps he had an eye on Sarojini himself? She did not want to be ousted as Sans Souci's courtesan, there were perks that went with the job, not to mention the fame and notoriety if the mark ever burst. It could be that he was getting fed-up of this quiescent lump of flesh beneath him, but it was not her fault if he liked to do it that way. If that was the case, she could soon remedy that. She could wind and wind like a ball of twine or let him have it roast fowl or head and tail or even from behind.

She put out a tentative hand to explore his spent genitals and test her thoughts.

Roger slapped her so hard her ears were still ringing when he left.

6

The rainy reason made a dramatic entry. It started foreday
morning, with no warning of thunder, as if it had raced the
sunrise and won. It came roaring across the hills in cutting
swathes of white, blotting out the greenery. It made a sound
like a continual crackling, as when they burnt cane for
harvesting. In less than a minute the hills were covered, and
then the sound approached the village, and a forerunning
pitter and patter plonked and pinged and splattered on the
leaves, and left small dark blobs on the asphalt road. Early
risers scuttled for shelter as it cataracted out of a leaden sky.
In one swift moment there was water everywhere, gushing in
the drains, cascading off roofs, swamping the road. Some
taxis on the main road pulled aside and stopped at the sudden
reduction of visibility, their windscreens battered and tattooed
to make wipers useless. Yards were flooded and water lapped
into huts. Fowls and goats, dogs and cats came in for shelter,
but the ducks swished their tails, thrust their necks to and
fro like pistons, and flapped their wings and stretched them
up so that even the undersides were soaked.

Dummy, naked, exhilarated in the open, lifted his head to
catch the tingling drops in his mouth. He ran willy-nilly,
splashing and kicking sheets of water, unable to understand
why others were not enjoying the world at this time: he had
it all to himself and it was too much for him. He cavorted and
jumped and pranced and lay in the road and rolled. He
played boat race by himself, dropping twigs in the drain and
watching them rush for the lead as they swirled away. He
climbed small trees and shook the branches to make more
rain. By and by it settled down to a steady roar which made
background for watery sounds: the gutters gurgling and
spilling their own cascades; the thatched roofs drip-dripping;
an empty can pinging as it collected the drops from a leak;

ducks quacking in the yards; the squelch of wheels on the road as traffic resumed slowly.

It fell for more than two hours, the first shower of the rainy season. It never let up during that time. Then, with a startling suddenness, the sun burst through the gloom with a patch of brilliant blue. Abruptly, at the height of its intensity, the rain ceased, with no warning, with no weakening or faltering or last lingering drops. It went as if by wave of hand and the sun took over with rapid stride and a high-noon concentration. Wraiths of steam rose from the earth, and a white mist on the hills disappeared and the freshened greenery shone. Only the weighted leaves in the forest dripped their last drops, and the gushing drains died to a trickle. Clouds panicked from the sun and the blueness of the sky stretched to the horizon in all directions. In a short time it was as if a passing cloud had merely paused to drizzle a piss on Sans Souci.

Dummy, drying out in the sun, scanned the sky for rainbows, but the change had been too quick and fierce. He sketched his own, his hands etching the air. He made an upside-down one, so that the ends touched the sky and the arc brushed the hills, and gave it to God as a present.

He did not expect anything in return, but later, that afternoon, he got something he had always wanted. At a blind corner of the village road, where it curved before coming to the temple, someone had left an old Ford car to die and be buried. Who did it, why, and when, no one knew, but it stayed there and was ruthlessly picked to pieces until only the body remained, a rusty hulk with peeling paint. The hood, through constant usage, was moulded into the shape of a man lying at rest. When the rich have worries they could go and lay on a psychiatrist's couch. In Sans Souci, when a villager was weighed down by circumstances, he went and lay on the hood. The human-shaped mould was shiny with use. He had a choice of distraction.

On the other side of the road, in a small field of oranges and tangerines, there grew the massive samaan tree casting shade; overhead was sky and cloud; and from up or down the road he could see the life of the village being enacted with a small bird's-eye view. The wreck was a positive danger to traffic, being at the ultimate part of the curve and invisible coming or going. After some grumbling and cursing of the unknown culprit's mother's arse, it had become accepted, and even, in a perverse way, welcome. It stopped all those bitches who drove like madmen killing stray dog or chicken: it particularly gave strange drivers a sweaty moment when they were flying along the road. Paradoxically, the danger minimized accidents. There were narrow shaves, and the facing side bore scrapes and scratches, but nothing serious had ever happened. The villagers were only waiting for it, for a death or two, so they could exclaim: 'I always know blood would of spill in this corner! Now the government got to tow it away!'

Apart from its therapeutic properties the junk afforded a playpen for children, who climbed through the open windows and doors, stuffed the headlight holes with leaves, and stamped about on any spot which was not dented. It was a practice drum for would-be drummers: they beat it with sticks and stones until it had lost all pretence of a musical note and could only emit a dull, dead thud.

It was here that Dummy was sitting that hot, windless afternoon, trying to see how long he could stand the burning metal. Even a weather expert like him was caught completely unawares by the freak gale that leapt out of nowhere, lifted him off the hood, and sent him flying to land in the hibiscus fence.

Dummy was so shocked he lay there paralysed for a minute, stunned by the unexpected flight. He had always longed to fly like a bird, and now that it had happened, he could not remember the sensation.

When he understood he got out of the broken hedge and grinned at the sky with his rat-teeth. That morning he had given God a rainbow. Now God had given him wings.

The earth was spongy on the estate after the morning rain. Fierce as the sun was, it could not penetrate the layers of foliage sheltering the cacao, but the rain had trickled down the trees and flowed where the land sloped, making little streams to join the drainage system which protected the estate from floods.

Too much rain was just as bad as too much sun for the cacao. Prekash had the men cleaning the drains, not only of dry branches and leaves, but wild growth. They should not have been blocked in the first place if he did his overseeing duties properly.

Roger woke during the rain and went back to sleep with a thin cotton blanket. In the rainy season it could be rather cool, especially when rain fell in the night. In the morning he made a note to have the gutters on the roof cleared . . . he could tell from the chatter of water they were blocked.

He was alone at breakfast . . . Garry was sleeping late. The new day minimized any urgency he might have felt to have a talk with Garry about Sarojini. First, he would have to decide what he personally was going to do about the situation. But at the moment all he felt like doing was saddle a horse and ride in the cacao and catch the glistening aspect of the vegetation before the land dried.

'Mr Roger!' Eloisa broke his thoughts. 'What wrong with you this morning? You only eat one bake?'

She had done fried bakes and scrambled eggs for breakfast.

'I know, I know, I have to keep up my strength for the hot sun. But it rained this morning.'

'All the more reason. You getting like Mr Johnson now, eating like a bird. I had to remind him that love don't full your belly . . .' she trailed off, realizing she was taking liberties, and covered up her confusion by dishing out more of the scramble for Roger, ignoring his warding-off hand.

'What love are you talking about?'

'Nothing Mr Roger.'

'Eloisa.'

She knew that tone. It was rarely used, but it instantly put their relationship in perspective. She stood stiffly.

'Him and Miss Sarojini.' The 'miss' was only out of respect for referring to Mr Johnson and the girl in the same breath.

'You listen to too much gossip.'

'Yes Mr Roger.'

'Just because Mr Johnson is seen with Sarojini sometimes is no reason to wag your tongue.'

'Yes Mr Roger.'

'He's collecting material to write a book, and she is only helping him to move around and meet people. You understand?'

'Yes Mr Roger. I must be getting crack in the head, to talk nonsense this bright and early morning.'

'I really can't eat all that, Eloisa.' He shoved the plate away.

'You got to.' She was back on safe ground. 'All that dampness outside. And you better take your cloak in case the rain come sudden again.'

He met Manko sitting on a bag of cocoa waiting for the men to turn out and the truck to come for loading.

'Morning Manko.'

'Morning Mr Franklin. Heavy rain, eh?'

'Yes.'

'Too heavy. The weather not turning proper. After yesterday I would of swear it wouldn't rain today.'

'Even you can't tell always.'

'Is not a good sign. Something in the air.' Manko waved vaguely. 'Something floating around that making me suspicious.'

Roger grunted. 'Don't forecast more rain.'

'Even worse.'

'What then?'

'Storm. Hurricane, maybe.'

'Chuts!' Roger had picked up the expression of disdain from the workers. 'We haven't had a hurricane for years.'

In fact, he had never experienced one, missing the last by a few months on his arrival in the island. It had left Sans Souci in ruins and that was why he got it at a bargain.

'Is about time for another. It going to be a bad day, Mr Franklin.'

'I'm not in the mood for your fancies this morning, Manko. Saddle a horse for me.'

The smell of cocoa was strong in the shed. Roger checked the bags, stacked almost to the ceiling. He picked up some loose pods and rubbed them to bring out the rich aroma. The crop had come mainly from his first planting, ten years ago. He had since sown another lot, but they were still young. It took five years for the trees to mature and yield, and after that, barring the dreaded witchbroom . . . the parasite that was the bane of all cacao estates . . . it was only a matter of maintaining them and reaping the harvest before the trees expired after twenty years or so. There was also his secondary crop of citrus . . . that should bring in a good return, particularly the grapefruit which had yielded well that year and was in great demand for the canning industry.

When Manko brought the horse Roger whistled for Rover and went down into his estate, the dog yapping and running ahead.

He spent the whole morning riding about. It grew exceedingly hot at midday, and in the afternoon not a breath of wind stirred. Steam rose like mist from the sodden ground and hung, creating a stifling humidity. Birds hid in the bushes, and the trees hung petrified with not the slightest tremble of a leaf or branch. The yard was deserted. The last truckload of cocoa had left and the workers skulked in the sheds, sitting or lying about on the cocoa bags. Someone had wheedled a tray of ice from Eloisa and there was a bucket of cold water from which they drank before it could become lukewarm. In the kitchen, Rover sat panting in a corner, lapping from a dish of water Eloisa had put out for him.

In the office, the electric fan hanging from the ceiling directly over Roger's desk packed up: the blades slowed down from a blur to a halt, as if they had finished a journey.

Roger looked up after a minute, missing the whirr and the warm air it circulated. He flicked the switch on and off a couple of times but nothing happened. He cursed. Every window in the house and office was open, but it made no difference. Behind him a large section of the wall was trellised for ventilation, but there was no draught of air.

He was very irritable. The day hadn't improved. Eloisa had made a *sancoch* for lunch . . . a kind of soup with a variety of heavy, starchy vegetables and ochroes and salted pigs' tails, allowed to simmer until the liquid was thick and slimy, with a *congo* pepper dropped in whole and unbroken to impart its unequalled flavour. He had gorged after his morning in the cacao, with a good appetite, but now the heavy meal was resting uncomfortably on his chest.

He could not make head or tail of the figures Prekash had entered in the books. The overseer had his own system and was usually there to explain his methods. But he had gone to pay the workers, and give the women time off to do their shopping and settle their bills.

He pushed everything aside on his desk and started to fan himself with a folded newspaper. There was a knock on the door and Ramdeen came in.

'I could see you a minute, Mr Franklin?' He stood there twisting an old felt hat in his hand. It was the first time he had been in the office and he wanted to get out as quickly as he could. It didn't seem such a good idea to tell Mr Franklin about Sarojini. He wished Prekash was there to give him courage.

He started from the doorway as if he had no intention of coming any further, 'Is about Sarojini,' but moved forward as he spoke.

It is pleasurable to drift the mind on the possible goodies when one expects a windfall. But useless delay to speculate on the nature of unfortunate circumstances when one *knows* something untoward exists. When Roger saw Ramdeen he did not wonder why he was there. He could quite simply say, 'All right, Ramdeen, don't worry, I'll attend to it.' That would abort so much embarrassment for Ramdeen, and leave himself some esteem. But like an actor on a stage he had to perform a scene. What Ramdeen was going to disclose . . . what he was disclosing even as Roger was thinking . . . had to come as a shock to him. He had to pretend, as master of Sans Souci, that he had no idea, otherwise he would have taken immediate steps. He was bitter that he had to reduce himself to this deceit.

But in fact, he did not contribute much, he turned his back and stood looking through the trellis, his mind far back in time, trying to bolster himself that what was past was gone and forgotten, and that if this was a fallacy and events landmarked the future, then he should be able to manipulate with some degree of control.

Once he got going, Ramdeen found he could go on and

on. He was talking now about how other coloured races might feel great to be touched with white skin, but it wasn't like that at all with the Indians, that Sarojini was bound and 'bliged to marry into her own race.

'East is East and West is West, and never the twain shall meet,' he concluded, quite pleased that he had manoeuvred his speech for this ending.

A strange thing was happening in Roger's mind. Even as Ramdeen droned on, Roger was enacting the scene with entirely different dialogue.

RAMDEEN: I find out about Sarojini. I had my suspicions all these years that she wasn't my daughter. Don't play you don't know.

ROGER: I've no proof that I am responsible Ramdeen. Kayshee never told me.

RAMDEEN: It can't be anybody else but you, You and Kayshee used to be just like Mr Johnson and Sarojini, behind my back.

ROGER: It wasn't like that. Let me explain.

RAMDEEN: I don't want to know the ins and outs.

ROGER: We don't know for sure. That is why I never did anything about it.

RAMDEEN: Except to sweeten me up with money from the post office every month, Don't think I didn't have my suspicions all the time that it was you.

ROGER: I only did that because I wasn't sure. I still don't know.

RAMDEEN: Just because you white, and you is a big estate owner, ain't give you no rights to treat people like that, Mr Franklin. You think we don't have feelings too? We got to decide what we going to do about this business.

ROGER: I am thinking about it.

RAMDEEN: Thinking don't *do* anything, Mr Franklin.

And he did not even remember having dismissed Ramdeen until he say him out in the yard, and he shouted, 'I tell you, man, there's no proof she's my daughter!'

'I don't blame you,' Garry said, coming in with a tray of cold drinks, 'I'm going mad myself. What sort of day is this?'

Roger moved to a barometer on the wall and tapped it.

He stayed so long that Garry asked, 'Well?'

'Nothing seems to be working around here.'

'I am. Or was.'

Still Roger remained where he was, composing himself before he faced Garry. He took a deep breath and it was like taking in a chunk of the heavy atmosphere.

It was at this moment that the freak gale struck the big house and snapped his thinking like a dry twig, sweeping everything from his mind.

Windows flew off their hinges and a series of bangs and crashes resounded through the house. The chandelier in the dining-room didn't swing on its chain, but was lifted up bodily to smash into the ceiling with such tremendous force it shattered into a thousand tinkling pieces. Spikes and globes and beads of crystal, complicated patterns of intricate design, squares and circles and triangles and prisms . . . all vanished in a twinkle. What remained fell back with a heavy jerk on the chain, and a few fragments dropped on the table as it swung a little before losing momentum.

'Oh God oh!' Eloisa stood trembling in the kitchen door-way, her head following the slowly-swinging wreck. Even more stunning, now, was the silence that came after the whooshing sound of the gale. Then outside, fowls began to cackle, Rover barked, and a babble of voices came indistinctly from the terrified workers.

In the office, Roger said, 'Jesus Christ,' and rushed out with Garry close behind. Roger put out a restraining hand as he saw the floor strewn with broken glass. Eloisa was still looking up, and though the chain had stopped moving her head continued to swivel.

'Let's get outside,' Roger said urgently. It seemed the safest thing to do.

It had come and gone with the speed of a bullet. The men were arguing what it was, and looking about for signs that it had really happened.

They saw Roger and Garry and rushed up, led by Manko. Roger tuned in to Manko in the confusing talk.

'Anybody hurt?'

'None of we,' Manko said, 'but Prekash was down in the cacao.'

132

'That looks like him coming now,' Garry said, gesturing. Prekash was puffing, and almost incoherent with terror. He had thought the experience was directed to him alone by some malevolent spirits until he saw the others.

'What happen Mr Franklin?' He stammered.

'Only a strong wind. Gale, rather.' Roger looked about for signs of damage and was surprised how normal everything appeared.

One of the men said, 'Manko say it going to have a hurricane.'

'There was nothing unusual about the midday weather forecast on the radio,' Roger told Manko.

The men were quieter now, even laughing. No one could imagine the fury of a hurricane in the lifeless atmosphere.

But Manko was concerned. 'Look at that sun, Mr Franklin. You ever seen it like that before?'

It was a dull red, and a brazen aspect to the sky had turned the blueness almost white. Yet there were no clouds, nothing that looked like a threat. It was only oppressively hot; most of the men had taken off their shirts.

Roger was controlled, but uneasy. 'I'll check with the Met station,' he said.

'You wasting precious time.' Manko shrugged. 'By the time you start to hear forecast, it might be too late.'

But Roger only told Prekash to keep the men and wait, and he returned to the office with Garry.

He sat on the edge of his desk and dialled, drumming his fingers as he waited for the connection. 'Hello. Mr Fraser, please. Roger Franklin. Hello Bob? What the hell are you boys up to?'

Garry tried to read his face as Roger listened with an occasional thoughtful 'Um.'

'What's up?' Garry asked as he hung up.

'I'm not sure. Bob's the best man at the station and he hasn't a clue. In fact, apart from the excessive heat, they don't know anything.'

'You mean that gale only blew *here*?'

'Apparently it was an isolated freak wind. I wonder if old Devertie felt it? He's just over the hills.' As he spoke Roger was dialling Devertie's number.

'Did you feel that gale a little while ago?' Roger asked when they had exchanged greetings.

'Gale' Devertie sounded amazed. 'No breeze blowing here at all.'

'We had a terrible blow. Smashed windows and almost blew us off the map.'

'That's funny. Nothing happen here.'

'It just came and went. A bit unusual, isn't it?'

'Why you don't phone the weather people?'

'I did. There's no information from them. Do you think it could mean bad weather . . . hurricane?' He added the last word abruptly.

Devertie took his time replying. He had detected the concern in Roger's voice and wanted to be helpful. 'I don't know,' he said at last. 'Might be. Those things happen so suddenly that you don't have a chance to sit down and take notes, so that when it happen again you will know what to do. I not trying to be funny, if you see what I mean. Best thing is to keep in touch with the meteorological station, you don't think?'

'Thanks.' Roger put down the phone and looked at Garry.

'I'm not going to take any chances,' he said grimly, 'and be sorry later that I didn't act.'

'What's to be done?'

'We've got a drill for a hurricane emergency on the estate. I'm going to behave as if this thing might really happen. Come.'

They went out again, to find Manko urging the men out of their complacency.

'That's right,' Roger told them. 'I want action, and quickly. You all know what to do. Every window and door nailed down. Everything put away. I want as many young cacao trees staked as possible!'

'I start to do that this morning,' Manko said, 'but none of them would help me.' He turned to them. 'You all believe now that this ain't no joke?'

'No more talk,' Roger said. 'There won't be any warning if a hurricane is around, and we have to look after ourselves.'

As the men moved off to various duties, Garry asked: 'What about the village?' He was thinking of Sarojini. One of the few times they were not together this thing had to happen.

'Let's concentrate on the estate,' Roger said shortly. 'Perhaps by the time we finish here we may get some news on the radio or something.'

'What can I do?'

'Go to the house and help there. And listen out for any news on the radio. I'm going to be busy out here. If you hear anything let me know right away.'

Dummy came tearing round the side of the house sending the fowls scattering in the yard, and collapsed in a breathless heap on the kitchen steps. He had conceded the difficulties of flying in the bush and had put away his wings for the time being. He took a short cut that skirted the front of the house so he did not see the great activity taking place as Sans Souci was battened down. But he found the kitchen door with two great pieces of timber nailed diagonally across it. It was a two-piece door . . . cut horizontally, the top portion serving for window, the bottom usually shut to keep out stray animals and insects. Dummy always clambered up and poked his head in to frighten Eloisa. But now he had to hammer for admittance, and even so he didn't see how Eloisa could open the door when it was nailed down from the outside. He found a chink and peeped through, and saw her sitting on a soapbox, her head in her hands. When he pounded the door, she looked up, frightened. He picked up a long twig and poked it through, wagging it about. Rover sat up and growled, then moved to the chink and sniffed and whined.

'Sic him, Rover, sic him!' Eloisa cried, but the dog wagged its tail, smelling Dummy.

'You not no watchman for me,' Eloisa said crossly.

She approached the shaking stick with caution.

Only God in heaven knew what was happening in Sans Souci today. The house was upside down with barefoot workmen stamping all over with muddy feet and disorganizing the whole place. They had had trouble to get in in the first place: she held them at bay in the passage with a broomstick and would not yield them an inch in spite of Prekash's protests. It was not until Garry came and explained what was happening that she grudgingly let them in. After that, as if spiteful for her constant vigilance, they began to wreak havoc with order and cleanliness, bringing in ladders and tools, pulling down curtains, dragging furniture and leaving marks in the polished floor, ripping pictures from the wall, and even going upstairs into Mr Roger's room.

'Hurricane!' she shrieked. 'Is better you-all let the hurricane come inside, it would cause less damage. Mr Johnson! Talk to these savages and cannibals!'

'Not now, Eloisa. We'll be careful. Why don't you go into the kitchen, out of the way?'

'Oh God! Now you want to drive me from the house!'

There was a yell from Prekash as a splinter from the shattered chandelier got into his foot and he began to hop about in pain.

'I wish you dead of blood poisoning. I would of left all those splinters to *chook* up all-you foot if I did know you was coming in!'

She began to store away vases and bowls and dishes, sparkling brandy and champagne glasses, ornate jugs and pieces of silver cutlery which were rarely used and mostly decorated the sideboard. While they tramped about she salvaged what she could in the confusion, muttering imprecations on their heads. By and by she retreated to the kitchen, unable to bear it any more, and shut her eyes and ears.

They were still at it when Dummy came. It was only when he pushed his finger through the chink and Rover licked it that she realized who it was. She opened a small window just above the kitchen sink and he climbed in and she bolted it again securely.

'Dummy. You come to keep Eloisa company. *One* set of confusion going on on the estate today. I don't know if I coming or going.'

Dummy sat on the floor playing with Rover.

In all the hammering and banging the radio had been going at full volume, mainly with music, in the background. Now there was a break in the music, and Garry shouted for silence to hear what the announcer was saying. By the time the noise abated his first words were lost.

'. . . No cause for immediate alarm. Precautions will be broadcast from time to time. Inside you should remove hangings and fixtures and store drinking water. Make sure you have lamps or lanterns and candles . . .'

Garry did not wait to hear more. He sent Prekash to tell Roger, and went into the kitchen to check the water supply with Eloisa.

At sight of Dummy there, Sarojini came rushing back to his mind.

'Eloisa! How long has Dummy been here?'

'He only come a few minutes, Mr Johnson.'

He bent down and looked into Dummy's face.

'Sarojini?' He mouthed the name slowly.

Dummy nodded and grinned and pointed in the direction of the village.

Garry was very worried. It did not look as if he would be able to leave the estate now: there was still a lot to do. He thought of sending Dummy to bring her to the house, but that might be endangering both their lives if the storm caught them.

'Mr Johnson.' Eloisa was so scared she whispered. 'The hurricane coming in truth?'

'It seems so. Is there food in the house?'

'Plenty boxes of things in cans. But Mr Roger prefer fresh food.'

'Where are they, outside?'

'No. Under the dresser there.'

'Don't let Dummy go out.'

He left as he heard Roger coming in from the yard.

Eloisa clasped Dummy to her bosom. 'You going to stay right here with me. Don't fraid, Eloisa will look after you. Listen to the radio, they playing music to comfort we in our distress.'

Roger came back exhausted. They had been able to secure some of the young trees, driving in stakes to support them, but it was hard work. For one thing there were not enough stakes ready and time had to be spent cutting more. And for another, he was anxious to get back to the house to check on what was being done. When Prekash came with the news it wasn't unexpected. It was unfair to keep the men any longer: they would have enough troubles of their own now. He sent them off warning of the grave situation. It did not seem to him that they fully appreciated the disaster that threatened . . . no longer a threat, but a certainty.

It was now about five o'clock, but it was gloomy, with a heavy greyness, and the sky was red and murky. Now and again the wind rose and died down, as if testing for the blow to come. Roger knew they could hardly finish the things that ought to be done: they would begin something he thought ought to have priority only to remember another job that was as, or more, important. It grew dark swiftly and suddenly and they could do no more outside.

Only when they were having a break for something to eat did Garry mention his fears for Sarojini.

'There's nothing we can do,' Roger said. 'They've had some time to do what they could, and I'm sure emergency measures have been taken.'

'What's keeping it then?' Garry burst out impatiently. 'We just sit and wait?'

'And hope and pray,' Roger said.

The hurricane originated some hundred miles out in the south Atlantic, and moved north-north-westerly towards the island, attaining a speed of about eighty miles an hour as it first struck land. It spread out in a twenty-mile path and swept up the east coast bent on utter destruction of anything in the way. Older inhabitants who had an idea what to expect said it was like spitting in the ocean to take precautions, that the best thing was to kneel and pray, and stay kneeling until it was over.

Before the blow arrived a police van went round Sans Souci cautioning people to take refuge in the station or school where emergency centres were set up. Some who thought they had time to shelter a goat or a cow or attend to something outdoors never stood a chance. A few gathered in the temple yard with food and flowers to appease the gods. They refused to move and stood or sat around the *pepal* chanting and singing. They tied their livestock to the tree with ropes and chains. But the *pepal* only saw to itself. It stood like steel when the blast came, but the worshippers went like dry leaves, and the animals were swung the full length of their tethers so that they strangled before the ropes and chains snapped. The temple went down with no protest, no lingering beam or post. It just flattened out like a punctured balloon, and in offering such little resistance all its components stayed undamaged in themselves, as if, later, it could simply be pumped with air back into existence.

The *pepal* watched the destruction of Sans Souci with indifference. Only the giant samaan tree caused it any concern as it bent and twisted, not completely uprooted, but thrown at an acute angle as if it had started to follow the wind and changed its mind. It was to become a challenge for any villager to walk close by in case it resumed its topple to earth and crushed whoever was near. But it survived at that angle, leaning in the direction of the templeyard. Only the *pepal* stood between it and the temple when it was rebuilt, and another legend arose that too many sins would bring it crashing down to destroy both *pepal* and temple.

The great house, too, stood like a rock though it shuddered and creaked and groaned and made other strange noises. Sheets of galvanize went slicing through the air, leaving a weak spot on the roof, and adding a new metallic note to the cacophony as the loosened sheets flapped and strained to take off. Small buildings on the compound were swept away or ruined beyond repair: the next day Roger found the Land-Rover, which somehow or other had been left in the open, had blown into the forest to wedge, overturned, in a small gully. The immortelle trees, planted for protection, now did more damage than the wind as they crashed down and flattened every cacao in their path. Roger had harvested in the nick of time. He learnt later that the warehouse in Port of Spain where San Souci's crop was stored was completely destroyed, and was thankful that he had already been paid and absolved from all risks.

For all their superstition, no villager would have credited the sight as the roaring gale with titanic force actually caused a part of the flooded river to flow backwards for a minute at a spot where it levelled off from the hills.

Eloisa swayed with Dummy in her arms singing, 'Rock of ages *cleff* for me,' in the kitchen.

Her voice quavered and rose and fell fearfully as she tried to drown the sounds of the storm, and in particular a whistling which came from the chink Dummy had pushed his stick through. She had tried to stuff it with rags but they kept falling out.

When she wasn't singing she kept up a disjointed conversation with Dummy as if the deaf boy could materialize words into pictures.

'Dummy, don't fraid, Eloisa will look after you. You ain't got ears, otherwise you would of heard the calamity and catastrophy that going on here tonight. I don't know what going to happen to we. Lord have mercy on a poor sinner. I have sinned against Thee, I confess my transgressions and my trespasses, I am weak and frail. Rock of ages *cleff* for me! When this storm going to finish? Why Mr Roger don't stop it? Rover, stop walking about like a restless spirit, you making me nervous. You hear that Dummy? You hear that big bang? Life if a tree fall down on the poor house! But don't frighten, Eloisa will look after you.'

Roger and Garry sat in the dining room. They had started a fresh bottle of rum, and talked about most things except what they should have been talking about. There was nothing to do. Once Roger got up and tried the dead telephone like a man testing a wet-paint sign. Now and again radio announcements struggled through a terrific batter of static.

'. . . High winds estimated at close on eight miles per hour. Hurricane Jenny is moving in a northerly direction. There is no news from Mayaro or Guyaguyare or other eastern coastal areas which were struck at approximately seven o'clock by the first gales. Telephone lines are down in most districts and we appeal to keep the existing lines free for emergency use only. Go to your police station or school if you are in serious trouble . . .'

Garry had the sensation that the house was like a ship in a storm, active and kicking and moving through heavy seas.

The whooshing outside had settled to a steady, relentless roar, neither increasing nor diminishing.

He was very tired, but his mind was feverishly active. He wished he could shape his thoughts and discuss everything with Roger . . . Sarojini. Manko's wizardry with the aloes, his work, his imminent departure from the island. Christ.

But it was Roger who took the lead. He too had milling thoughts, and as if coming to a decision he briskly poured a drink and topped up Garry's.

'Is it serious about Sarojini?' He asked, stuffing his pipe.

'Yes.'

That was it then. One short question, one short reply.

Garry said, 'I was just going to tell you about it.'

'You'd better listen to what I have to say first. Sarojini may be my daughter.'

Garry fought his immediate reaction and thought, in Sans Souci people change into animals at night, children walk with their heels forward, men divined the future and healed sick people with bush medicine, possession of a *corbeau's* egg ensured prosperity, and Sarojini is Roger's daughter. Check. With a little time he should be able to reconcile himself to this more human and understandable circumstance.

'You said "may be"?'

'Yes. Because I don't know. I've kept this to myself for years. It's a relief to tell you. Are you shocked?'

'I can't think.'

'Sarojini's mother . . . Kayshee . . . used to work on the estate. She was very beautiful.' Roger's voice lost tenseness as he went on. 'She was never in love with Ramdeen . . . you must have heard how the Indians marry their children off at an early age. Hers was like that. He treated her badly. She used to show me bruises when he beat her in his drunken fits. He even did it sometimes on the estate until I interfered.'

'Because he knew?'

'Nobody knew. We couldn't enjoy the freedom you and Sarojini seem to have had. Well, there you are. I was never sure . . . Kayshee never told me anything, and Sarojini looks so much an Indian, it's hard to believe she might have white blood.'

'You just left it like that all this time?'

141

Roger shrugged. 'I made arrangements for Ramdeen to get a monthly allowance, providing he didn't marry her off. It seemed the most I could do at the time. Gladys was still alive . . . she died shortly after. I just let the whole business drift, until I heard about you and Sarojini.'

That was possible too, Garry thought, and said, after a while, 'There must be some way of making sure.'

'I suppose so. A blood test, or something.'

'I wonder if Sarojini ever feels anything.'

'She's not to know, Garry. This is my business and I want to sort it out myself. Don't confuse the issue by telling her or dropping any hints.'

'Everything is all mixed up and spinning in my brain.' He wanted to assimilate slowly, a gradual process isolating each thought for separate consideration. Given time, one could believe everything in this valley: *douen, soucouyant,* Manko, *hole in the head,* Sarojini.

'Do you know something,' he said, unnaturally loud, 'I haven't heard *one* calypso since I came to Trinidad.'

Roger looked at him curiously.

Eloisa came in then and stood some distance away, and said something in a frightened voice which they did not seem to hear. She repeated:

'Mr Roger! The hurricane going?'

As if in answer, through the restless crackling and pistol shots of static the radio announced a report from the Meteorological Station stating that the eye of the hurricane was due to pass over the northeast area, that the winds would die down suddenly, but that the lull might only last a few minutes.

'Stay in safe shelter. We repeat, stay in safe shelter as the eye passes over your area. The hurricane is likely to increase again from the opposite direction with full force . . .'

'What eye the radioman talking about, Mr Roger? God coming to inspect?'

Apparently the lull had started some time, but they were so preoccupied they did not notice.

'It's only temporary,' Roger said. 'It may be worse when it returns.'

'I notice since about half a hour that it not making so

much noise. Thy rod and Thy staff, they comfort me.'

'How is Dummy?' Garry asked.

'He sleeping Mr Johnson. I spread a cocoa bag under the dresser, and he curl up there with Rover as if nothing happening.'

'What about a nice hot cup of cocoa, Eloisa?' Roger suggested.

'Yes, it will give me something to do instead of waiting and waiting. Rock of ages, *cleff* for me, and Mr Roger and Mr Johnson too.'

They did not talk again for some time, because they had so much to think about. Eloisa came back and put the steaming cocoa on the table, made to speak, observed their tense silence, and went back without a word.

Garry was about to say something, merely to break their silence, he had no idea what he might have said, when Roger raised his head sharply.

'Did you hear that?'

'What?'

'Sounded like someone pounding on the outside door.'

'Sarojini.' Garry rushed out even as Roger was looking for a more logical reason.

The banging was muffled but regular and insistent. By the time Roger joined him he was wrenching the boards away from the door. He had only taken a few pieces away when the wind hurled one side of the door inwards with such suddenness it struck Roger across the arm.

Prekash staggered in and they quickly battened the door again. Garry felt a sudden dread and his heart beat fast as they took Prekash to the dining room.

He was in bad shape, shedding water and mud and wet leaves as Roger led him to a chair. His breath came in great gasps, as if in between them he didn't breathe. Something seemed to be wrong with his left hand as he clutched it to his heaving chest: the wrist was broken.

Roger filled a glass with rum. 'Here. Drink this.'

But it was some time before he could recover sufficiently, and Roger had to hold the glass to his mouth.

'What happened?' Garry could not wait.

'Give him a chance,' Roger rebuked.

'Not a hut standing in the village,' Prekash said, and began to laugh.

'Prekash,' Garry said, 'listen to me. Where is Sarojini? Is she all right?'

'He's suffering from shock, give him a chance,' Roger repeated.

'Sarojini.' Prekash spoke the name without meaning. His fingers crabbed the table cloth nervously: Roger held his broken wrist still.

'Where is Sarojini?' Garry spoke slowly.

'She gone.'

'Where?'

'She gone to Garry at the big House.'

'Oh God,' Garry said.

'Wait,' Roger was calm. Prekash's eyes did not seem able to focus on anything. 'Was she with you? Where is she now?'

'Gone,' Prekash said. He seemed preoccupied with his broken wrist.

'We won't get any sense out of him . . .' Roger began.

'I'm going out,' Garry said quietly.

'Don't be crazy. You want to get killed? Wait until we can get some sense from him.' Roger slapped Prekash.

'I know she's out there somewhere.' Already Garry was filling a small flask with rum. 'Don't try to stop me.'

'You'll only kill yourself.'

But Garry was already on the way out.

'It's madness, I tell you.' Roger went after him. But even as he protested he was in the kitchen searching for a cutlass and a coil of rope.

By the time Garry had freed the door, Eloisa was standing near, wringing her hands and praying, and Dummy and Rover came to watch.

Roger thrust a powerful torch and the rope and cutlass, all quickly bundled, on Garry.

'It's hopeless in that wilderness. We could organize a search party. You don't know where she is.'

But even as he went on Garry was out, stepping into pitch darkness and lashing rain.

Before Roger could nail down the door, Dummy and Rover dashed out after Garry. Eloisa screamed.

Roger took her back to the dining room. As he made a rough bandage for Prekash's wrist, she knelt down and began to mutter endless prayers.

Sarojini was in the school on the main road when the eye of the hurricane passed over Sans Souci. In the comparative lull, the cries of woe and misery and wailing children were accentuated. Two men who had been delegated to maintain some sort of discipline in the bundles of stricken humanity were moving from group to group repeating the same words monotonously . . . that they were not to leave the building, that the hurricane was still blowing.

No one was interested.

All thought had been driven out of Sarojini but the one that she should have been with Garry to die with him. She sat huddled and alone, unaware of the misery surrounding her, unaware of Prekash who had been casting glances in her direction from time to time.

She did not even look up when he came to her.

'Sarojini. As if the hurricane stop.' He sat next to her and put his arm around her shoulders.

'Sarojini. It stop a little bit.' In his own fear and shock he could not help but be bitter that even in the tragedy he could not get her to respond to him. He removed his arm.

'What you say?' She jerked a little.

'It stop, but it going to come back.'

She did not speak again, but she sat up a little, and as if conscious of his nearness, inched away. They sat like that for a minute and then before he knew what she was about, she had risen and was stumbling over the listless bodies on the floor. He thought she was going to pee, but when he looked again she had disappeared.

'Sarojini!' He jumped up.

It was from then that the gap in his memory occured. He never knew he followed her. Death was expected and nothing worse could happen to him. As he fought his way through the bush he was prepared for it. The desire dominated him and made him blind to every peril and obstacle. It assured him that he would catch up with her, it assured him that he would have her trapped between him and the raging earth.

But when he grabbed her and flung her down, there was no lust or anger or frustration to motivate him. He was just propelled by an irresistible force into a dark, fumbling world and he was so sad and desolate that he cried as he tore at her, shed tears as he ripped at her, sobbed and strained to push her legs apart, whined like a lost pup and grabbed more mud than flesh from her wild, resisting body.

He was never to know the rape was not granted, that he was doomed to the perverse pleasures of imagination only. Long afterwards, when he tortured his memory to recall some aspect of the ravishment, he found he could remember nothing at all from the time he jumped up in the school, and he used to spend hours sitting and staring at the wrist that had been broken. The bone had set unevenly, with a little bump he was forever rubbing lightly with his fingers, as if the contact helped to focus his imagination on all the lurid details reality had denied him.

A man who knows his capabilities and his limitations is benign to Papa Bois and the spirits of the forest. That night if Garry had gone out raging and waving his sword, with hopes of victory and conquest, he might have met quick, ignoble death. As it was, he was almost humble in his hopeless inadequacy. Also, he was frightened as hell.

He lost much strength in his panic and despair trying to hack his way through solid walls of fallen trees, before realizing it was more expedient to skirt the masses of impeding jungle. Had it not been for Dummy and the dog, he would have never found the track. All around them the forest noisily protested with snaps and crashes and heavy thuds which shook the earth. Several times he wanted to give up . . . not to return, but to fling himself down and surrender. He did not know where he was or what he was doing. He lost all idea of time and distance. Once, with the torchbeam slicing the solid darkness, he saw Dummy walking ahead of him like a *douen,* facing him yet moving away.

It was Rover that found her while they were skirting an enormous immortelle, completely uprooted so that it seemed to be growing upside down, its branches stuck in the mud and its roots above the earth. She was pinned by a stout branch almost buried in the mud. Miraculously, smaller branches had plunged into the earth and seemed to have cushioned the contact of this main stem.

He did not pause to investigate her condition. Giving Dummy the torch to hold and direct, he attacked the branch wildly with the cutlass. He was slashing at it for some time before he realized he was making no progress. Time and again the blade stuck and he had to tug it free with both hands. He forced himself to be calm. He discovered that the limb was not rigid, it yielded to pressure. In his panic he might well have caused it to bear down more on the girl. Acting with some care now, he attached the rope and passed the other end around a branch for leverage. He indicated to Dummy what he was trying to do, so the boy could pull her clear if he managed to shift the weight off her body. His feet sank in the mud as he strained at the rope, and he could make no purchase until he awkwardly braced them in a fork near the trunk of the tree. As if he did not have enough to suffer, a new thought came to panic him: how were they going to get back? Nervous sweat mixed with his wet hands and they kept sliding on the rope. Then Dummy stuck the torch in a fork after broadening the beam, and came to his assistance. This time the branch bent, and taking the strain, Garry quickly secured their end on another limb. Then he moved her gently, until she was clear of the clinging mud. He had no presence of mind to search for injuries or consider the risk of moving her. He only remembered the flask of rum and forced some into her mouth, and a little seemed to go down.

Rover, sniffing at the spot where her body had been, met instantaneous death when the taut rope broke loose, the branch snapping back to crack his spine in two.

Garry tried to lock Sarojini's arms about his neck, but one hand was clenched tightly, and when he forced the fingers open he saw Manko's donkey-eye.

How he found the strength to carry her back . . . how

they managed to reach the house at all . . . he was not conscious of, only staggering after Dummy, the *douen*, as the boy turned with the torch and actually walked backwards at times. Later he was to learn that Roger had defiantly switched on the generator and the house blazed with light to guide them back.

Garry was shaking and trembling and unable to give any coherent account of what happened. But Roger did not waste any time with questions. He examined the girl and as far as he could tell there were no broken bones or visible signs of injury. He got a little more rum down her, and she showed fluttery signs of returning consciousness. He and Eloisa took her upstairs to one of the bedrooms, and he left Eloisa in charge: the old woman was more in control of herself with something to do.

The lull had only been a break for the hurricane to amass its forces of fury, for it came back with a magnified power that had the house straining to keep upright. They were the most frightful hours that Roger ever experienced. He did not even have the companionship of Garry, who huddled with his arms and head sprawled on the table. Prekash just sat there with glassy eyes, looking at his bandaged wrist as his scattered thoughts tried to make a connection.

By and by the house grew still of human sound: even Roger fell into a kind of doze.

Dummy crept upstairs and found Sarojini. He knelt down at the side of the bed and burrowed the rest of his body to nestle against her. He did not sleep, but the soft comfort of the mattress and the clean white sheets was a wonderful sensation, and he knew that his best friend would be all right. He stayed with her until the pale ghostly light of foreday morning filtered weakly through a crack in the window, then he got up and left the house.

A fine drizzle was falling, so fine it was almost invisible and more felt than seen. He could see nothing he recognized. As if a raging, demented giant had trampled through the night, everything was broken, askew, flattened, scattered in bits and pieces about the compound. He wandered through the desolation of fallen trees and slanting shrubs . . . it was as if the hills had been magnetized and tried to pull everything towards them. The utter lifelessness depressed him greatly, it was a new sensation for him, not fear, which he knew, but a dead hollowness which made him feel empty inside, and at the same time heavy with oppression.

He could not see a roof or a post standing when he got to the village, and the weak, insipid light cast a sorrowful aura of permanence through the misty drizzle, as if the world had gone dead and would never come to life again.

7

Sarojini opened her eyes, a mere flicker to confirm life, and shut them again. There was a faint, pleasant smell of cedar in the room, mingling with *veteeveh*, a straggly root people put in clothes cupboards to keep the linen fresh and fragrant. She could hear the murmur of running water in the gutter, a trickle amplified by the stillness of everything else. Only people in the tropics know the music of this sound, and only in bed, after a night of heavy rain, can it be appreciated. It is a purling, soothing sound, easing the awakened senses into the new day, evoking imagery of earth washed clean, flower and leaf polished to display colour *for so.*

Sarojini did not know that this morning it belied the broken world outside, that it was a dirge and not a foreday lullaby. Before her befuddled thoughts could get direction she fell asleep again, her fingers curled on the donkey-eye.

Downstairs, Garry and Roger were trying to face the enormous breakfast that Eloisa had produced. She was back in stride, in high spirits. Outside there might be calamity and confusion, but praise the lord, her dear house was still standing and they had a roof over their heads. Soon the sun would chase that stupid yeah-yeah drizzle away, and it would be just another day. The men would have a lot of work to do, and before they left the house she was going to see they had their bellies filled.

The radio droned with news, a dreary assessment of death and destruction. The path of the hurricane had been narrow, but vicious and devastating where it struck.

'Come on, Mr Roger. I not going to let you and Mr Johnson leave the table until you eat up all your breakfast, hurricane or no hurricane. You will need all the strength you have today.'

They were impervious to her cheerfulness and cajolements,

and after a while she left them, clucking like an outraged hen.

Garry had peeped in and seen Sarojini asleep before he came down. He had thought a shower would revive him and ease his heaviness of heart, and was naked in the bathroom before he discovered that the shower was not working. He had to slap the pipe and keep shaking it to get any water, and in the end compromised by washing his head only, and rubbing down with a little Limacol, a soothing lotion made from limes.

He did not talk much with Roger when he came down. For one thing, there were so many decisions to make, and things to discuss, not the least of which was his return to England in a couple of days or so. He had refrained from telling Sarojini the exact date because it was one of the many considerations that they had kept putting off. She hushed any talk that threatened their happiness, trying to make their days together into a forever love. Now, too, there was a feeling of guilt that he was due to leave the valley when it was down on its knees from the hurricane.

Roger decided to leave the estate alone for the time being, and most of the day they were in the village helping the rescue parties. It was a grim business. A few houses near the main road were still standing, and were used as stations to bring in the injured and dead. Survivors were too dazed to be of much assistance to the voluntary workers who had come from other districts which were not as badly destroyed. But some of them were in the temple yard, round the *pepal* tree, and incredibly, there were already offerings of food and flowers, and attempts to put the temple together again even though their own huts lay in ruins.

By midmorning the sickening drizzle was dissipated as the sun forced a way through the grey and gloomy atmosphere. There was no wind to shift the clouds, but a small circle of blue spread out like a ripple, pushing them away. Steam rose like a mist, shrouding the village as it licked its wounds.

That evening Roger got through to Devertie when he found the phone working.

'A terrible business, Mr Franklin.' In the aftermath of the disaster the old man's voice still had a kind of dignity and quiet authority. 'I try to get you a couple of times today.'

'I was in the village. How are things with you?'

'Bad. You?'

'I haven't been looking yet, but I expect the worse.'

'Here today, gone tomorrow. I suppose you suffer more than me, because of the hills. What about your men?'

'Picking up the pieces in the village.'

'You didn't keep them on the estate?'

'No?'

'You should of kept them in the big house, they would of been better off. I had my men here and their families too.'

It hadn't occured to Roger to do that. He remembered now that he had gotten the impression that the villagers had expected something of that sort: there was a kind of respectful reproval in their attitude, and uneasy, he had arranged with the shopkeeper to let them have whatever they wanted at his expense.

They spoke a little longer then Roger went to join Garry for a drink and to persuade him some more that it would not help things if he postponed his departure, that it would give them both a chance to sort out the confusion in their minds and make decisions about the future.

When Roger and Garry left the house that morning, Eloisa took a hot cup of cocoa up to Sarojini.

'Sarojini! You sleeping?'

'Eloisa?'

'Yes. Here girl, sit up and drink this. It will do you good.'

'Eloisa! What happen? What I doing here?'

'Mr Johnson rescue you from the storm last night and bring you here.'

Eloisa sat tentatively on the edge of the bed as Sarojini sipped the cocoa, then jumped up quickly and smoothed the sheet where she sat. Unusual things were happening, but that was no reason for her to forget her place in Mr Roger's house.

'I don't remember nothing, Eloisa.'

'Nothing at all?'

'Only when I left the village to try and come here.'

'You was mad to go out in that storm, girl. You might of kill yourself.'

'Garry! Garry all right?'

'Yes, fret about yourself. He and Mr Roger gone to the village.'

'Eloisa! I better go before Mr Franklin catch me in the house, in this room sleeping!'

She started to get out of bed but Eloisa pushed her back.

'You not to left the house. That is the orders.'

'I shouldn't be here, Eloisa.'

'Fly your kite high while you could, girl. Both the white men say you is to stay here. Must be until you better.'

'Nothing wrong with me. Look.' Sarojini flung the sheets aside and got up. 'You can't expect me to stay in bed all day, though is the best sleep I ever had.'

'Come in the kitchen then, and keep me company.'

They went down and Sarojini had something to eat. But she was anxious to get out, to see Garry, to look for friends and neighbours and find out what was happening.

'Sit still and don't fidget so,' Eloisa said. 'The whole house in a mess, if you want to do something you could help me clean up.'

'Yes Eloisa, anything. I would go mad unless I have something to do.'

The morning passed as she busied herself about the house. The sort of cleaning Eloisa had in mind would take months. She wanted to turn everything upside down, shift the furniture about, change the whole appearance of things. As Sarojini scrubbed the floor, she went on a tour of inspection so she could report to Mr Roger.

It gave Sarojini pleasure and satisfaction to tidy up Garry's room, and she lingered over the job. It was while she was arranging some papers on a small table near the head of his bed that she came across the passage ticket. She almost passed it by but the large, colourful envelope attracted her curiosity and she looked inside.

Eloisa found her sitting there with the envelope dangling in her hand, slumped in dejection.

'Oh God, you see the same thing? You witness how I tell

this girl to stay in bed and she disobey me? What Mr Roger going to say? What Mr Johnson going to say?

She got a bottle of bay rum and chafed the girl's face and hands. She made Sarojini go back to bed, keeping up a stream of scolding talk about the dangers of relapse, and actually pressed the girl's eyelids down to make her sleep before she left the room.

Garry got back to the house before Roger, exhaustion almost overlapping his depression and concern for Sarojini. But he went straight upstairs.

She was sitting up. She had found a comb and brush and done her hair: the long, shining tresses dominated her appearance and made her look frail. He took her in his arms and she clung to him, great sobs shaking her so that he had to hold her tightly to steady her.

'It's all right.' He patted her back as if comforting a child. It's all over now.'

'Garry, Garry, Garry.' She hid her head in his chest, and he stroked her hair with his chin. She kept repeating his name as if it was all she could say. He felt it was delayed reaction to the night's ordeal; he did not know her anguish was in discovering how soon he was leaving her. Even if the hurricane had destroyed the whole world she did not care, but it had come and created a beginning for Garry and herself, and their ending loomed swift. He talked gently, saying he should have stayed with her, but there was so much to do in the village. 'How are you feeling? We ought to have a doctor.'

But she only called his name and sobbed, he could feel his shirt wet with her tears. Several times he tried to let her go but each time she tightened her hold fiercely.

'You'll need all your strength to get well. Rest now and I'll ask Eloisa to make you something, one of her special broths. I hear your father . . . Ramdeen . . . broke his hand and is in hospital. Dummy's all right.'

He kept up a light, disjointed talk, but she did not seem to be listening. She held his hand, stroking it and watching the movement. Her eyes were bright with tears. He took his hand away gently and pressed her back on the pillows, promising to return in a while. Still she said nothing, and when he turned at the door she looked the other way.

Eloisa made her a fish broth from the head of a grouper, simmering it with butter and a sprinkling of herbs and the juice of fresh limes, and refused to be put off, spoon-feeding the listless girl when she would not touch it herself.

Evening had settled peacefully on the estate when Roger joined Garry, already having his second rum punch. It was such an evening as his first, and they were sitting in the back veranda, Garry in the rocking chair. It was hard to imagine the destruction around them. Moonlight softened the hills, and the rain had brought out croaking frogs that kept up a chorus in the drains, one group signalling another when it was about to stop, passing the sound around in all directions

Both men knew how necessary it was to come to an understanding. They had made contact and there should no longer be any need for reserve or reticence. Yet, there had been no whole-hearted exchange. With typical English restraint they dwelt each in his castle, disliking intrusion, minimizing disclosure.

Roger was irked by an illogical feeling that Garry had brought bad luck to Sans Souci, and things would only fall in place when he left. He did not want to be forced into personal decisions by the actions and motives of anyone else.

'How is Sarojini?' He asked.

'She seems all right. We ought to talk about things.'

'Well, I told you. It's best to get back to England and give yourself a chance to think. You might even be able to forget it all.'

'No.'

'But you're going?'

'I suppose so. I haven't told Sarojini.'

'She'll forget too.'

'No.'

'Anyway, it will give you both a chance to sort yourselves out.'

'I could take her with me,' Garry said weakly.

'Sarojini in London, walking down Oxford Street, surviving in the winter? She'll be lost if she ever leaves this valley.'

'There are drawbacks to everything.'

'It won't be fair to her. Look Garry, let's try to be firm

about a few things. There is no reason why you can't come back to Trinidad . . . Sans Souci . . . if you both feel the same way after separating.'

'I suppose there's that.'

'You might even come into the cocoa business with me, though I'm in a bad way at the moment,' Roger went on quickly, before they were distracted from one unsettled issue to another. 'And you don't have to worry about Sarojini. I'll keep her here, at the house.'

'What are you going to do about that?'

'I'll clear the matter up. There's so much to do.'

Garry sighed. 'It's a very scrambled arrangement. I feel nothing will be the same again, as if the hurricane swept into our lives and threw everything out of gear.'

'It's only a coincidence it happened just before you're leaving.'

'You think so?' There was a lot he could argue about, but now their love was reduced to banal level, to welcome and good-byes, to doubt and misgivings, to fears and tears. 'I'd better tell Sarojini.' He got up. 'She's the only one that matters, and she doesn't know a thing.'

'She must know you had to leave some time. Why stretch things out?'

'I suppose so.'

She was awake in the darkness and when he called out softly she said, 'Don't put on the light, Garry. Come.'

He went in and got into the bed as her hands guided him. He began to say something but she put her fingers on his lips.

'Don't say nothing. Not yet. This is the first time we ever in a real bed together, Garry. All the time I was imagining what it would be like. Don't say nothing. Just lay still.'

The darkness, and the warmth of her body, eased his mind. He relaxed. She stroked his face and hair, and kissed him without passion.

'So you going, Garry, so soon. As if the hurricane come to take you.'

She kept one hand on his mouth each time he tried to speak.

'I seen the boat ticket in your room, that's how I know.

But I not crying, Garry. You see me crying? I know you had to go one day, even though we never talk about that. And I know why you didn't tell me before, because you thought I would of cry. Not so? But I not crying. You see me crying? You and me don't have to talk, Garry, because we know what we have in our minds. Other people, they have to explain, and make excuses, and talk talk talk all the time, when they could be making love. We didn't waste no time talking, Garry. It ain't have nothing I want you to tell me, I don't want to know anything, or to ask you any questions. I won't love any other man though. I won't let no other man touch me when you go, as long as I live. I want you to promise me one thing, though. Don't talk. Don't try to tell me how you feel, or what you will do, or what I will do when you gone. You promise? I know you think I will cry, Garry, but I not crying. You see me crying?'

When the distraught villagers went to see Manko, they were not surprised to see the obeahman's hut still standing. It only strengthened their faith in him, that he had powers beyond their understanding, that he could defy the raging elements while lesser mortals were brought to their knees. They did not come for magic spells and charms, but to learn what the outlook was for tomorrow, now that they had lost all their possessions, and to ask him to get in touch with departed spirits. It was too early for that, he said, the poor spirits barely had time to leave the bodies, three days had to go by before he could attempt anything. And besides, the gods were still in an angry mood, and it would be dangerous to approach them now. As for the future, ah, it depended on if they changed their ways. The hurricane was a punishment for *thiefing* and cursing and fornicating and thinking evil, and didn't the news say that Sans Souci was the worst-struck village? They should go and mend their ways. He himself was under penance because he thought he could challenge what had been decreed. He wasn't going to call any names, but a man had been marked for doom and he, little Manko, had shaken his fist at the sky and tried to turn the will of the gods. For that, they had wiped all his magic off the face of the earth . . . and he pointed to the spot where his shed had been. He was going to be out of business for some time as his hands were tied without the tools of his trade.

Earlier, about the time Garry and Roger were in the village, he picked his way about the estate assessing the damage. The smell of cocoa and oranges and tangerines pervaded the dank atmosphere. The spongy earth was strewn with crushed fruit and battered shrubs and fallen trees. What vegetation remained looked as if a dozen bulldozers had run amok. Here and there were swathes of light where still stood a few lucky immortelles, but the landscape was like a pack of cards that badly needed shuffling. The river was swollen and muddy. Its course through the estate was winding, and in several parts it was blocked with driftwood and tangles of weed and grass. There were tributaries to it now which never existed before. Where it was sluggish and shallow and piled up to form islets of broken bamboo and uprooted shrubs, a small horny-scaled fish, the cascadura, sought shelter. They would be plentiful now with the start of the rainy season, and hungry villagers would fish for them wherever the sticky, frothy substance of their eggs showed on the surface. Experts merely pushed their hands in the mud and caught them, but the best way was to stir up a fluster and back them against the bank and cast a small net. The catch was strung on pliable lengths of bark and hawked about the village or on the main road, the fishermen squatting patiently in the hot sun waiting for customers from the plying traffic. The cascadura is still alive hours after it is caught. It looks lifeless, and only moves if it is disturbed by touch. The flesh has a coarse texture and the taste of a sardine. In pre-war days it was only eaten by poor people in the country villages. but now it appears on the stalls of the city market and fetches a handsome price.

Manko learnt from Eloisa about Sarojini's rescue when he went to the house. As usual he did not appear to seek information but Eloisa was bursting to divulge all the news. She did not wait to enquire how he had survived before going into a long and colourful description of the night's events at the house.

Manko listened indifferently. It seemed to him the hurri-

158

cane marked the end of his evolvement with the affairs of Sarojini and Garry. He had nothing more to divine. no advice to give, no opinion to express. What had to happen would happen. Sarojini had made her bed and had to sleep on it. After the dance and the song, it was time for retribution. Nobody ever got anything for nothing. He was tired preaching it, people would never learn.

Sarojini visited him the morning after she had slept with Garry for the first time in a real bed. Some deep strength she did not know she possessed had helped her to hide her feelings from him. It had its roots in her love, and it was as wondersome to her as to him, because she had thought she had nothing more to give and this thing blossomed in her and made silence more precious than words. When she stopped him from speaking, she knew the harrowing and despair he was going through. They had never spoken much, why should he be tortured now? Words only translated their love to a harsh reality and took away the magic and enchantment.

But it needed Garry's presence to sustain detachment. Once in Manko's hut she broke down and wept and moaned, rocking to and fro as she squatted on the ground, her hands clasped diagonally across her breasts to keep her body from falling apart.

'What I going to do when he gone? Tell me, tell me.'

'I got nothing to say.' Manko shut his ears to her lamentations.

'Do something, Manko, do something. You got great powers to help you. Stop him from going.'

'Why? You getting on as if you didn't know all the time he had to go.'

'Sudden-so, Manko, sudden-so!'

'You would think it sudden even if he stay another ten years. Best forget this whole business, child. It had *maljo* on it to start with. I warn you and I warn you, but you didn't listen. Nobody does listen when things going sweet.'

'How you expect me to forget Garry, Manko?'

'I could give you something for that. You won't remember nothing.'

'No!'

159

'Well, remember then, if you want.'

'You think he will come back, Manko? He promised to come back.'

'Well then. Stop moaning.'

'He going to come back quick-quick, and we going to married.'

'You lucky.'

'I really don't know why I crying. It only going to be a few weeks. You think he will come back, Manko? Look in the sun and tell me. Please Manko please.'

'Even if I could look clean through the sky I won't. You ain't learn your lesson? Go and make an offering to the *pepal* tree and ask Vishnu or one of them Indian gods to help you. You can't see the hurricane take away all my obeah? I doing penance for trying to help you, and that white man who don't have no faith in the spirits-them.'

'Ah Manko. Oh. Even you driving me away. I got nobody, I got nothing.'

But Garry was thinking of her at that moment. It would have been selfish and callous to stay with her when there was so much to do in the village, and though Roger was prepared to excuse him he went along. He was grateful for Sarojini's fortitude, but ashamed that she had been the one to display courage and self-possession. After they loved in the bed he allowed him to speak, and they had whispered in the darkness about all the things they had not done or said, and pretended that it was as well for it gave them more to look forward to when he returned, it would be like meeting for the first time.

The news of his leaving quickly got about in the village, though he said nothing himself. Roger had told everybody, and when he was having a drink with Prekash in the shop, the young overseer regretted that they could not throw a big farewell fete for him in the village.

Prekash was elated and showed no animosity. He had told the village that he broke his wrist trying to save Sarojini in the hurricane, that he crawled to the big house for help, that if it wasn't for him, she would have been dead and buried in the bush. And indeed, if he had not risked his life, how would Garry have known she was out there? This was the aspect he polished and embroidered for the public. And now, Garry was going, and he would have Sarojini all to himself. This time he wasn't going to make any mistakes. One day, one day, congo-tay! And to crown it all, Garry was the one who had saved her for him! She would come crawling on her hands and knees now.

He insisted on paying for the drinks, and said, 'I know you was going, Garry, but not so sudden.'

'The quicker I go, the quicker I can come back.'

'Oh, you coming back?' That didn't bother him.

'Yes. Look after Sarojini for me, Prekash.' Her wholehearted surrender to him had left no doubts in Garry's mind that Prekash meant nothing to her.

Prekash spluttered his drink and turned his guffaw into a cough.

'You couldn't left her in better hands, Garry.'

Dummy came into the shop while they were talking and Garry beckoned him. He was fond of the boy and wished there was something he could do for him. Perhaps when he came back he could arrange for him to be examined by a specialist. He wanted to give him a gift and wondered what he would like. The shop stocked a variety of odd things apart from groceries.

He lifted Dummy to stand on the counter and indicated the shelves.

Dummy did not hesitate. He pointed to some small fishing nets piled in a heap. The shopkeeper brought him one and Dummy inspected it carefully. Just the thing to catch cascadura in the river. Perhaps Garry would join him. He went into a pantomime showing how he would use the net.

'You going to catch cascadoo, Dummy?' Prekash called the fish by its local name.

Dummy tugged at Garry, pointing in the direction of the river.

'You go on, Dummy.' Garry shook his head.

As Dummy bounded out of the shop, Roger came in and joined them, and the conversation turned to the problems on the estate, and how soon Prekash and other workers could make a start there. He already estimated that he would have to have extra labour . . . they might need a bulldozer, or at least a tractor. At the moment the contractors who had these might be busy on more urgent relief work, but it was wise to make arrangements for their services as soon as possible.

Dummy went to the house, picking some of the hardier flowers to take for Sarojini, making a bunch and carrying it in his new net like a catch of fish. He hoped she would be well enough to go with him. But when he met Eloisa, she told him Sarojini was not there. Eloisa took the flowers and put them in a jam jar on the dresser, wildly making signs to assure Dummy she was only minding them for Sarojini.

Dummy, regaled with hot cocoa and a thick slice of home-made bread liberally spread with butter and guava jelly, set out to try his new net. Two were better than one at catching cascadoo, but he could not lure Eloisa to accompany him, and in any case, it was young and beautiful Sarojini that he wanted.

He found her crying in Manko's hut when he stopped off on the way to the river.

'Look at that boy,' Manko said, as Dummy was hugging her and wiping the tears on her face, 'and take example from little children. He can't talk, he can't hear, he can't even walk true-true backwards like a *douen*. Count your blessings, girl, that you wasn't born like that, and stop moaning about things you can't change.'

'Garry going, Dummy, Garry going away!' She turned her sorrow on the boy, holding him so tightly he couldn't display the fishing net.

'Is time you stop crying, girl. Here, drink this.' Manko gave her a little rum in a cup. 'The world not coming to an end, though it ought!'

But nothing he could say comforted her. He had resisted the temptation to give her some visible token, or pretend to perform some magical rite to put a spoke in the wheel of her destiny. But it was better to be harsh and stern: one day, congo-tay, she would be grateful to him for his representation of reality.

'Do something, Manko, do something.' Even Dummy could not halt her grief as he spread out the net to show her.

'You going to catch cascadoo, boy?' Manko asked.

Dummy pulled at Sarojini and gestured to the net and the river.

'Go with Dummy and catch fish. It will give you something to do. You know what they say about the cascadoo. If you eat it you bound to dead in Trinidad.'

He spoke idly, without significance. Her worry about Garry might have brought that childhood memory back to him. He wasn't sure afterwards, he kept thinking that perhaps a pattern formed in his mind at that moment . . . Sarojini grieving for her departing lover, Dummy there with the fishing net to catch the cascadura, and he wanting to give her some symbol, some assurance that would stem her sobbing. Or it may have been he just wanted to get rid of her.

Whichever it was, in reality it worked out different. Sarojini looked up and said, 'What you say?'

And he brushed it aside. 'Some stupidness about the cascadura. You don't remember when you was in school it had some stupid poetry we used to learn. Why you don't go with Dummy and left me in peace.'

Sarojini sat up straight and stared directly in front of her, as if at some invisible presence, and intoned: ' "Those who eat the cascadura will, the native legend says, wheresoever they may wander end in Trinidad their days".'

'I didn't say that,' Manko said uneasily. 'You best remember that, Sarojini.'

'The native legend.' She trembled as if possessed. Her grief had vanished, the tears now polish to make her eyes shine. She spoke the verse again as if the words were put in her mouth.

Manko shook her roughly and her head wobbled as if it had no control. 'Behave yourself,' he said sharply. 'It was only a joke I make.'

But something was happening in the hut. In all his years, whatever spirits were evoked, whatever obeah was created, had been through his instrumentality, and he had been in command of the situation. Now spirits were being manifested, taking shape, mobile as smoke drifting in the air, and he had no idea where they came from, or why. It was as if Sarojini was caught in a trance, in an enchantment that excluded him. Dummy saw something too, he put out his hands as if catching bubbles.

Manko was frightened. Some old people used to say that it was looking for trouble to deal with obeah and call up the dead to aid the living, and that sooner or later a man wouldn't know what was real and what was caused by spell. The shapeless images, really like drifting smoke, were sinister and foreboding. He had a feeling that if he concentrated he would see a vision, a message.

Then Sarojini combined a shriek and a laugh and stood up and chanted, 'Them who eat the cascadura got to dead in Trinidad!'

From extreme sorrow to extreme joy. She laughed and took the fishing net from Dummy.

'Listen girl,' Manko said earnestly as she returned to normal, 'it was some stupid Englishman what say that. White man don't know nothing about obeah. Even the people in Trinidad don't believe that foolishness.'

'Touch the net Manko!' She thrust it at him. 'Put a little *zeppy* on it to make it catch plenty!'

'You will catch nothing but trouble.'

'Come on Dummy.' She pulled the boy out of the hut.

'Remember what I tell you, Sarojini!' Manko called after them. 'You dreaming another dream what going to collapse and leave you worse off than before!'

But a wild hysteria was upon her. She saw a pattern in the boy with a net, in Manko's careless recollection of the legend, in the flooded river teeming with cascadura at this particular time. Everything from the beginning had been tinged with magic and omen, and now she had got a sign to stretch the ending, to put it out of sight with the hope that Garry would come back and they would create a new beginning.

She was anxious and impatient. At the first sight of the river she wanted to fish. She had never done it before, she thought it was only a matter of casting the net and pulling it in. But Dummy restrained her and led her to the hidden spot where she had spent so many happy hours with Garry. This reinforced her desperate hopes, especially as Dummy went there of his own volition. And again, there was more wonder when they got there, for by some miracle the spot had escaped the brunt of the hurricane, and there were still oranges and tangerines standing, and the torrent from the hills had been diverted. The stream had not overflowed the banks at this point, but the water was muddy and the sides clogged with bamboo and odd debris.

Dummy showed her what to do. They held out the net between them and splashed and beat the water, moving towards the bank, driving the cascadura before them to seek refuge in the mud and under the islands of driftwood. They closed in the net slowly, and while Sarojini held it Dummy went down on his knees and pushed his hands into the mud where the fish wriggled to bury themselves.

They could have taken the fish away in the net itself, but Dummy wanted to do it the proper way, and he strung them on strips of bark, selecting the largest ones for Sarojini.

Eloisa was preparing the evening meal when they got back to the house. She looked askance at the fish Dummy proudly displayed.

'Don't bring them nasty cascadoo in my kitchen,' she sniffed, stopping them at the steps.

'You self Eloisa,' Sarojini reproved, 'these is fresh fish we just catch.'

'Too much trouble to clean,' Eloisa grumbled. She touched them as if afraid to soil her fingers. The fish jumped and she put her hand to her nose and made a sound of disgust.

'Fumm!' she exclaimed. 'They smell fresh! I done have dinner to prepare, you know.'

'You ever taste a good curry-cascadoo?' Sarojini asked.

'No,' Eloisa admitted, 'and Mr Roger well like his little curry now and then. But I can't make it like you Indians. I wanted to ask you to teach me.'

'You got everything I need? You got a massala stone?'

'Yes. Look under the dresser. But don't clean them fish in my kitchen! Look a basin, you could sit down on the steps and do it.'

Dummy picked fresh limes for her from a tree in the back, using a long bamboo rod. She sat on the steps with a sharp kitchen knife and gutted the fish. She cleaned them thoroughly with the limes, and left them to soak in the basin with some of the juice while she ground the curry ingredients on the massala stone, A feeling of peace and security came over her as she worked. She even hummed an Indian air.

'Hum,' Eloisa said, 'this morning your face was like sour tamarind because Mr Johnson going, and now it sweet like cane. What come over you?'

'Nothing.'

'Don't try to fool me! I know you went to see that old vagabond Manko. He must of given you some medicine to drink. You shouldn't take anything from that rascal.'

Sarojini laughed. 'You know the history? If you eat cascadoo, you bound to come back to Trinidad!'

'Oh-ho! I know Manko would full up your head with stupidness. You think if Mr Johnson eat cascadoo he will come back, eh? Poor you, Sarojini!'

'Not Manko say so.' Sarojini was not dismayed. 'The Native Legend. You don't know about these things, Eloisa. It was a white man, a visitor just like Garry, who come to Trinidad in the old days.'

'Well, Manko or Mr Legend, it make no difference. I don't know nobody eat cascadoo and had was to stay in Trinidad.'

'Not stay. Come back. Garry could go and roam the whole wide world, but he got to come back once he eat that fish. You understand?'

'And supposing after all this trouble he don't eat it?'

'He will eat it when he know I cook it specially for him.'

'Better him than me. Manko must of well give you some *zeppy* to put in the pot. You won't catch me eating it. It might make me disappear or something!'

'I didn't put nothing. You want to taste?'

'No thank you. I will stick to my breadfruit and saltfish.'

Later, when the sun was westering and not so hot, she went with Dummy to the village, keeping away from the scenes of activity where she might come across Garry. She did not want to see him just now. But she stopped at the *pepal* tree to leave some flowers and a small enamel plate with some

of the cascadura which she had brought as an offering. It
would please the spirits in the tree that she had not forgotten
them. She prayed for a minute, and promised that this was
the last time she was going to bother them with her petty
problems, from now on she would try to behave like a
responsible person.

Dummy left her and she went to see Kamalla, and found
her sitting on a fallen mango tree shelling pigeon peas from
a basket.

'Sarojini! I hear you nearly dead in the hurricane, girl!'

'I still alive.'

She sat down and began to help shell the peas without
being asked, as they talked.

'You see what happen to we village, girl? You know your
father in hospital with a break-hand?'

Kamalla did most of the talking, giving her all the news,
and then she said, 'But what about you? I hear that Garry
going back to England day-after-tomorrow. Troubles come
by the dozen, girl.'

'Oh, he will come back.'

'You think so?'

'Yes.'

'H'mm.' Kamalla was thinking about Mr Franklin's last
visit to her hut, asking all those questions about Sarojini.
With Garry out of the way, maybe he would leave her coast-
ing and turn to Sarojini for his little comforts?

'You staying at the big house?' She asked curiously.

'Yes.'

'For how long, pray?'

'Until Mr Franklin throw me out, I expect. Garry say I
must stay at least until he leave, and after that, Mr Franklin
going to make some changes.'

So that was it. He couldn't even wait for Garry to go,
he had Sarojini installed in the big house already. She was
furious.

'What stupid changes?'

'How I should know? Garry didn't tell me.'

'You sleeping with Eloisa?'

'I got a room upstairs.'

'Girl, you really rise up in the world! That hurricane

bring everybody bad luck excepting you!' Kamalla curbed her jealousy, seeking information. 'I suppose you takes your meals with them too?'

'Don't talk stupidness. I tell you is only because of Garry that I allowed to stay there, because I ain't have no place to live.'

'You not the onlyest one!' Kamalla cried. 'Look at me. Last night I sleep on the floor in the school, like everybody else. And you allowed to traipse about in the big house like a *lady*! Is not you should be there, Sarojini. After all I do for Mr Franklin!'

'What you mean?'

Kamalla checked herself, breathing hard. 'You will find out soon enough. That innocent face you put on don't fool me, you know, Sarojini. It got more than the pestle in the mortar. I didn't fall off a tree.' In her agitation she tipped the basket and scattered all the peas.

'Look what you done with your foolishness. What come over you, the hurricane addle your brains?' Sarojini could see no reason for Kamalla's behaviour. She got up to go. 'I pick up myself and say I coming to see how you getting on, but if that's the way you feel,' and she shrugged to finish the sentence.

'Yes, you better go, seeing as you turn into this high-born lady now, and got no more time for your poor friends. But watch out, Miss Sarojini. When cock crow too loud he fall off the roost!'

She had hoped for some comfort and friendly conversation with Kamalla, but left with a feeling of dismay. Indeed, there was gloom in the whole destitute village and she did not tarry, but went back to the house.

She asked Eloisa, 'Eloisa, Mr Franklin say anything about me?'

'Like what so, girl?'

'I mean, I can't stay here. Nothing wrong with me again.'

'Which part you going to go?'

'I don't know. Somewhere. Everybody sleeping in the school.'

'I meant was to ask him about that myself. I thought you was going to stay till Mr Johnson gone? If Mr Roger didn't tell you nothing, what you worried for? Go and lay down, you look tired.'

She went upstairs, but she couldn't rest. Kamalla's outburst, and the state of the ruined village, made her realize she had nothing at all left, not even a change of clothing. In fact, it had been at the back of her mind to borrow a sari from Kamalla so she could wash the one she was wearing. Where was she going to live? Some vague apprehension of the situation had already come to her, but it only blended into her misery and despair. The visit to the village brought it to the forefront. She had promised to fend for herself if her last wish was granted, and it was not too soon to make a start. Even before Garry went she should have some idea of the immediate future. She was not at ease in the house, it frightened her somewhat and she moved on tiptoes on the polished floor and carpeted staircase. Perhaps if she asked Mr Franklin he might allow her to stay in the servant's quarters, with Eloisa? She could sleep on the floor. She could not encroach on his hospitality any more, especially as it was only because of Garry.

When Roger came . . . Garry had been delayed having farewell drinks with the villagers . . . Sarojini was busily polishing the dining table. Preoccupied as he was, he was half-way up the stairs before he realized, and stopped and turned.

'Sarojini. Eloisa can do that.'

It was the first time he had spoken to her; he came down slowly, giving himself time to think, and even so, undecided still about what he was going to say. He had avoided this meeting, waiting for a time and a place when he had threshed out all the complications.

'Are you feeling better?'

'Oh yes.' She kept her head down. She could see his reflection in the polished surface of the table.

'Good.' He turned abruptly to go.

'Mr Franklin?'

'Yes?'

'I was wondering, being as I have no place to live, I could stay by Eloisa for a little while and help out with the cooking and the cleaning.' Her voice faded out.

'Yes, yes.' He did not want to linger. It was all going wrong, he regretted each moment he stayed. 'That's all right. When Garry . . . Mr Johnson goes, there is something we must talk about.'

He went up then, as she shyly murmured thanks.

He flung himself in a wicker chair in his room. What a mess everything was in. He badly needed a drink, but didn't want to go down again and risk more talk. It nettled him that his movements were impeded in his own house, and if he rang for Eloisa like as not the girl would come. He lit his pipe and calmed down. He knew so little about her. If she stayed around the house a while, he would be able to observe her closely, watch her movements, detect some slight mannerism, some little idiosyncrasy that might indicate his blood in her veins: perhaps he really should have it tested. Though he had never given the matter much thought, he would never have imagined the position as it was now, with her already in love, and with someone like Garry. He did not want to make any mistakes by jumping to conclusions. Once Garry left, in his own way and time he would resolve things.

He yawned and tiredly dismissed her and considered what was to be done at Sans Souci. He had given two days to the plight of the villagers and could not afford to neglect his own business any longer. He remembered Devertie's suggestion about amalgamating the two estates. If it was ever to be considered, there was no time like the present.

He glanced at his watch. It was half-past six, time to have a wash and a drink and call Devertie before Garry came home for dinner.

He freshened up and sipped his drink as he telephoned. After they were talking for a minute he mentioned the idea.

'You want to sell up?' Devertie sounded surprised.

'Definitely not. I thought we might discuss the idea, that's all.'

'Any time,' Devertie said. 'In fact, I been worried about you. You done an assessment yet?'

'I'm starting tomorrow. I'm short of labour.'

'Listen. I know we ain't decide anything yet, but I could

lend you some men. We not so badly off in Maracas as you, and I know what it like when you down.'

'On what terms?'

'Terms?' Devertie was puzzled. 'We not talking business. We talking as friends. I could lend you some machinery too. A couple of trucks, and maybe a tractor.'

Roger felt the offer was genuine, and without strings. But he hesitated. He did not want to be obliged.

'Listen,' Devertie went on, 'if you want to wait until we meet, or we get our lawyers together to negotiate, that's going to take a lot of time.'

'We're not at that stage yet,' Roger said cautiously.

'I know you English people like to do things that way. But you don't have to commit yourself at all.' He paused. 'I'm glad you been thinking of it, though. I can see that hill that separating us even as I talking to you now on the telephone. It's a dream I have, to stretch over that hill. You stretch from your side, I stretch from mines, and we meet at the top.'

'And plant a flag,' Roger said facetiously, amused at the simple way Devertie put it.

'No. We build a great house as a sort of headquarters, overlooking all the land we have.'

'We'll have to build a road.'

'That too.'

'It's an idea. But at the moment I've got to get on my feet.'

'No rush. I got a few hundred young plants you could transplant from Maracas to Sans Souci. Listen, why we don't meet and have a talk?'

'All right,' Roger decided. 'Give me a few days to run over the estate, and I'll come to see you.'

'And my offer to help is good, however things turn out.'

After the conversation, replenishing his drink, he felt heartened by Devertie's concern and sympathy. Garry came in and went upstairs for a wash, declining a drink, saying the villagers had plied him trying to get him drunk.

In the kitchen, Sarojini warmed the cascadura over a slow fire, and when the men were ready Eloisa took out the other dishes. Sarojini did not want to go into the dining room, and Eloisa did not encourage her. In fact, Eloisa was beginning to have misgivings about Sarojini being in the house, fearful that she might usurp her rights and domain. It was pleasant to have her company for a while, but she hoped Mr Roger didn't have any ideas about keeping her around permanently.

'Sarojini cook something special for you all,' she announced when she took the dish in. 'At least, for Mr Johnson.'

'What is it?' Garry uncovered the dish and sniffed. 'Umm, curry.'

'Curry cascadoo.'

'Looks like sardines.'

'It's something like,' Roger agreed. 'I hope it isn't too hot?'

'She didn't put no pepper in it.'

'I haven't had this for ages,' Roger said, as Garry waited to see how he would tackle it. 'Take off the outer bony scales, like this.' He easily removed the shell of scales which enclosed the fish, revealing the succulent flesh.

Garry tasted a piece and said, 'It's delicious.'

They ate in silence for a while then Roger said, 'You've got this one for your book, of course?'

'What?'

'The cascadura. You're supposed to end up in Trinidad if you eat it, no matter where you travel.'

Garry thought it was just like Sarojini to produce something like this; he would ask her about it later. It was embarrassing to have her eating in the kitchen with Eloisa, but he did not see what else Roger could do at the moment. There were times now when he tried to imagine her in a mini-skirt, or drinking tea with her little finger cocked. But such pictures he deliberately blurred. He did not truly want to formulate impressions like these, there would be time enough when he returned. He wanted to remember her as a wild flower in the open, dancing the cocoa, laughing on the beach at Balandra, lying under the trees with the wind in the leaves and sunlight broken by green foliage.

Later, she was upstairs after dinner waiting for him to come to her.

'Let's go out, Garry,' she said. 'Is full moon, we could walk about the estate.'

'You not afraid of jumbies in the bush?'

'I not afraid of nothing with you.'

'All right.' He was glad to go, it was like making illicit love when they were in the house, and he suspected that for all her show she was not comfortable surrounded by walls.

He got Roger's torch and they went out, not without Eloisa's imprecations.

'The both of you looking for trouble!'

'It got moonlight, Eloisa,' Sarojini said.

'Better yet for them evil spirits to see you out there. The night-dew would make you catch cold, girl.'

But Sarojini was determined to be out. She had decided it would be the last time they were together before Garry went, and she wanted to be back once more at their favourite rendezvous by the river.

The shortest distance betwen two points is a straight line. The hesitation, the procrastination, the weaving in and out, the wrestling and the bewilderment, the loss of direction and the tentative uncertain groping in whirlpools of thought as the mind staggers to come to a decision, are all products of a civilized society to which people like Garry and Roger were prey. The colossal burden of a brain shuttling to and fro with no mission was not for someone like Sarojini. Once she had the vision of the cascadura, she acted upon it and left the matter in the lap of the gods.

It was not for someone like Kamalla, either. The more she thought about the situation at the big house, the more she was possessed by resentment and jealousy, and she did not hesitate to make a decision. Basic, natural forces, termed 'primitive' by a civilized society, were working on her. Artifice and subterfuge, subtlety and compromise, ploy of diplomacy and tact, were for white people and not the likes of her. She was not going to wait, or hope, or pray or spend wishful hours accepting or rejecting possibilities that might never be.

She made a flambeau, stuffing a rag in the mouth of a bottle of paraffin, and it gave a smoky flame, but threw enough light for her to see her way to the big house.

Dark shadows jumped at her, evil spirits pretended to be trees or clumps of bushes and snatched and tripped her up. The very moonlight, instead of allaying her fear, cast light

here and shadow there so she could not tell which from
which: once she froze as she saw a party of *douens* gambol-
ling and dancing near the very spot the village women had
performed their ritual dance, but she did not look too closely.
The best protection was to see but play as if you didn't see:
when a *soucouyant* flashed over the bamboos and disappeared
to hide and wait in the shadows for her, she made a small
detour. She stumbled on, shutting her ears to strange whis-
pers and a peculiar hooting which accompanied her all the
way. All these apparitions and noises were only being created
to put her off, but her rage left no room for the terrors of
the night.

Eloisa did not open the front door when she pounded on
it, but called out from inside, 'What that there this hour of
the night?'

'Me, Kamalla. Open the door, Eloisa.'

'Kamalla!' It was some jumbie trying to get in the house
because Mr Roger was out on the back veranda and couldn't
hear. Kamalla! 'Whatever and whoever you is, best hads go
away before Mr Roger come with his gun and shoot you with
silver!'

'I got to see Mr Franklin. You better open the door, you
stupid woman, before I break it down. Is me, Kamalla.'

Eloisa opened the door a chink and peeped. It looked like
Kamalla. 'Kamalla?' she said doubtfully. 'What you doing
here?'

'I tell you I got to see Mr Franklin.' Kamalla wedged her
foot in the opening.

'This hour? What about? Somebody dead?'

'You just go and tell him I got to see him right now.'

'Wait outside.' Eloisa tried to shut the door, but she was
no match for Kamalla. She came in and stood with folded
arms.

Eloisa said crossly, 'You should of come round by the
kitchen, you know. Give me the message and I will
tell him.'

'What I got to say is for his ears alone. You just hurry up
and tell him that me, Kamalla, here.'

Eloisa looked her up and down, said, 'H'mm, wait right
here,' and went away.

Kamalla thought of Sarojini surrounded by all this grandeur and ground her teeth. But soon it would be her turn to strut and play white lady, and drink cocoa-tea from them fancy china cups on the table instead of some nasty chip-up enamel mug.

Eloisa came back and said, 'He say you could come. But don't think you walking in here with any dirty foot. You got to go back out behind the house by the back steps.'

Roger's first thought was that something serious enough had happened in the village to justify this visit, and that Kamalla had been delegated to bring him the news.

As she came up the steps she rested the smoky flambeau on the bottom one.

'What's happened?' He rose from the rocking chair.

'I not good enough to walk through the house, eh? I have to come round the back like a thief?'

'What is it?' Her attitude was so unexpected that her words did not register with him immediately.

'I say I not good enough to come in the house, eh?'

Even then, he saw her only as a villager bearing a message, and said impatiently, 'Come on, what's the trouble?'

'You!' She laughed then, a jeering sound that made him frown.

'What's wrong with you?' Slowly he was noticing her wild appearance and the glitter in her eye. 'Have you gone mad?'

'Yes.' She laughed again, and he felt uneasy, and irritated at the feeling.

He used his voice of authority. 'All right, Kamalla. What is it?'

'You don't use that tone of voice when you come for a little piece!' She mocked him. 'You don't feel for something now? I could spread out on one of them beds inside same like Sarojini!'

'You must be drunk or mad. I don't care which. Just get out.' Roger was too civilized to cope with a primitive situation like this. He had no dialogue, no idea what to say or what to do. He thought if Manko was around he would get him to throw her off the estate.

'All right. You want me to go. But watch out when the mark bust!'

He was not deaf to the veiled threat nor what it insinua-
ted. He would be foolish to pretend outrage, or that he did
not understand.

'I will come to see you tomorrow,' he said. 'We will talk
about things then. Go now.'

'We going to talk right here and now!'

Her persistence unsettled him; he said, lower than was
necessary, 'What you want? Some money?'

'Guess again.'

She was taunting him, her mockery enraged him and he
realized that he should get rid of her quickly before he lost
his dignity completely. What had brought about this rebel-
lion? He had always been generous to her, not only for
services rendered but to ensure the utmost secrecy about the
liaison.

'You're a stupid fool,' he said. 'Do you think anybody
would believe anything you say, or take your word against
mine?'

'We will find out when I bust the mark, and tell the whole
world about the great white man what slink about in the
village to catch a piece of cunt!'

He struck her then, slapping her across the steps so she
pitched and stumbled and would have tumbled down them
if he did not grab her. It was a forceful blow which he
instantly regretted. It was intolerable that he should have
to suffer the humility she was imposing on him, but violence
was not the answer.

It might have been, had Roger augmented the blow with a
few clouts and kicks as any sensible Trinidadian would have
done, that he would have driven ambitious ideas from her
head. But such drastic measures were far from his mind.
Indeed, the situation had developed alarmingly in the two
or three minutes since she came, and he was terrified of 'a
dreadful scene.'

He was not to know that if in fact the mark busted, it
would not come as any great surprise to the villagers. True,
it would created some talk and notoriety for Kamalla. But
his prestige and standing would not be harmed, rather, the
men would approve and appreciate that white man or no
white man, he had to dip his wick now and then to keep

176

in practice, and Kamalla happened to be handy and was always bouncing her fat arse around, too. Some of the women might even wish they were the lucky one.

But Roger saw himself disgraced as master of Sans Souci by this ignorant woman.

'What do you want?' he asked, restraining himself with an effort.

The single blow and his quick repentance did nothing but increase her confidence. 'I want to come and live in the big house like Sarojini, that's what I want. I don't mind sharing with she. If you think you going to throw me away like some rotten calabash you very sadly mistaken!'

'Sarojini isn't living here.' The humility of having to make explanation to this common whore had his voice hoarse.

'Oh? That's not how I hear the story. I hear you bring she here to keep you company after your white friend go.'

'I've told you once,' he said, mustering his dignity and patience. 'Go now. And don't ever come back here!'

'I ain't moving a foot until I get satisfaction. All them times you straddle me like a beast . . .'

'Shut up!' He could barely hold back from striking her again.

'You sure Sarojini not staying here?' There was a whine in her voice now.

'Get out!' He could not stand much more.

'All right.' She began to move down the steps, and picked up the flambeau. 'I going to give you a little time to settle this business. And if you don't, the mark bust, so help me God.' She tried to make the sign of the cross with her forefingers and kiss it, forgetting the flambeau, and almost burnt her face. 'Just remember what I say.'

When she left he was trembling with a compulsion to strangle her. He poured himself a heavy drink and gulped it down.

That night he dreamt he was in bed with Sarojini and woke in a sweat. And grew thoughtful.

'If I could manage one day while you still here,' Sarojini said, 'it will help me to manage all the days you not here.'

That was why she wanted this to be the last time, in the same spot they had first made love.

'What will you do tomorrow, then?' He felt he had to make some protest, but in a way he was relieved.

'Oh, plenty things. I got to go to hospital to see my father. I got to look for my friends and see who alive and who dead. I got to start being independent, you know? I got to start learning how to live by myself until you come back. Don't try to find me. I won't come back until you gone.'

'I must see you before I leave.'

'No. This is the last time. I think my sari getting damp on this wet grass.'

'We should have brought something to lay on.'

'Eloisa would of thought we mad to go and sleep in the bush when we have that nice bed.'

'You're beautiful in the moonlight.'

'And when sun shining?'

'Yes.'

'You only saying that.'

'When I get to England . . .'

'Don't talk about England. I don't want to listen.'

'You should listen . . .'

'No. I cork my ears. Look.'

Communion with words was a new dimension throwing darkness where there was light, hinting at woe, remindful of drought and cold winter and loneliness and despair. It would slowly eat away and erode their precious, silent love, and they shrank from it, were even stilted in its usage.

So they lay in the moonlight, bridging gaps of silence with desultory utterances, or with fondle and kiss, stilling great fears in each other, cautious lest the spell be broken with a wrong word.

Sarojini told herself she would have the whole day tomorrow to cry and she must not give him any sign that might make him suspect there was a life beginning in her. She was not sure herself, but she would find out when she went to the hospital. She did not want anybody to know. She had been tempted to ask Kamalla, or Eloisa, but it would have been like sharing Garry with them. She did not want to think too much about it just yet, she was keeping it in reserve for when she was alone, so that the miracle, if it were true, could console her. Like how she skirted whatever attachment threatened the dream that was their experience, so she treated this possibility of bearing his child: it was one secret, the only thing she had allowed herself.

When they went back to the house they slept together, making sad love. Foreday morning, when he was sound asleep, she loosened the knot in her sari and took the donkey-eye and put in his hand, folding the fingers around it. She slipped quietly out of his arms and went away.

8

'Come, kip, k-i-p!' Eloisa scattered corn in the yard from the calabash, and counted the fowls as they came scurrying for their morning feed. Two leghorns were still missing, but there was a brood of chickens with one of the hens.

'Good thing you all born after that hurricane,' she told them, and threw some left-over rice, as they could not swallow the grains of corn.

She kept looking out for Manko, impatient for someone to talk to, so impatient that if he did not come soon she would have to talk to the fowls.

Yet when he came out of the cacao, she turned her back from force of habit.

Manko surprised her by talking first. 'I hungry, Eloisa. What you got to eat?'

She started to say something but changed her mind. He would listen better if she filled his belly.

'Come in the kitchen,' she said.

Quickly, she put some food before him, and before he could take the first mouthful she burst out, 'Manko! Sarojini missing! She gone since yesterday! Mr Johnson gone this morning! He left something for you! He left something for me!'

'Give me a chance before he start leffing things for everybody!'

'You don't understand! You realize Sarojini must of stow away on that ship with Mr Johnson? Bacchanal! Scandal!'

'Oho. So you is the one, you old *maco*.'

'What one?'

'The one always interfering in what don't concern you, and spreading malicious gossip.'

'Who, me? Which part she gone if she ain't gone after him on the ship? She love that man too bad, Manko. You should know. They must of plot that scheme all the time.'

'Sarojini ain't got no place to go. She will turn up soon.'

'I will believe when I see with my own two eyes.' It was such a juicy speculation Eloisa let it go with reluctance. She busied herself about the kitchen, waiting to see if he would ask for his present.

But Manko did not speak until he finished eating. Then all he said was, 'I got to go up in the hills today.'

'Here.' Eloisa took the parcel from under the dresser. 'Mr Johnson left a mosquito net for you.'

'What I will do with that?' He was indifferent to the gift. All he wanted was to forget the whole business. He was thinking about the estate, Sans Souci joining up with the Maracas valley. Mr Franklin had asked for his opinion, and he wanted to go up in the hills and walk around a bit. He wasn't sure about the terrain for cacao. Vaguely he remembered, even before Mr Franklin's time, that a survey had ben carried out and reported the land unsuitable. But these days there were hardy types of cacao which might thrive on the hillside.

He got up and shoved the parcel aside. 'You keep it. I don't want it.'

'He give me a bible. A *holy* bible.'

'You set up for life. A bible, a mosquito net . . . what else you could desire?'

'Don't be so disgrateful. You shouldn't refuse a present.'

He started to leave, and Eloisa's voice rose to a shrill. She harangued him as if she had prepared for it.

'Is all your fault, Manko! All this business! You and your obeah! You and your donkey-eye and your cascadoo! If you is this great obeahman you suppose to be, you should work some obeah and make people wishes come true, instead of dealing with the devil!'

As he went out she grabbed the bible and shook it at him. 'You should read the good book and pray that you get converted and set on the paths of righteousness!'

She was still fuming an hour later when Sarojini came with Dummy.

'Child! Where you been to?'

'Nowhere.'

'You hungry?'

'No.'

Eloisa gave Dummy something to eat. Sarojini sat down listlessly, expelling a great sigh.

Eloisa looked at her. 'Now girl. I just give Manko a piece of my mind. Now for your share. What happen done and finish with. Mr Johnson is a *big* white man what living in England, and he was only here on holiday, and the two of you like one another, and now he gone back to England. Crick crack, monkey break my back, wire bend and the story end.'

Sarojini said nothing.

'A-a, I nearly forget. He left that donkey-eye on the dresser for you. He say is yours, you must keep it, it will bring you luck.'

Sarojini stretched and took it and held it loosely in her hand. She wished he had kept it. She did not pay attention as Dummy took it away and put it in his pocket. He had another donkey-eye there already which he had found only that morning.

'Best make yourself busy, girl, instead of sitting down there like a poor-me-one. The yard want sweeping.'

Sarojini took the yard-broom and went out with Dummy. As soon as she had swept a small space, Dummy took the two donkey-eyes from his pocket and rolled them like dice on the clean spot, playing.

'Dummy! Where you get that other donkey-eye from? How I going to tell which is which now?'

She knelt down and stared in perplexity at the two seeds. They were so similar in every detail not even a great obeah-man like Manko could tell the difference.

She did not know which one to pick up.